# Anchor Murder

## *Doug Fletcher mystery #18*

### *Dean L. Hovey*

### Print ISBNs
Amazon print 9780228639015
Ingram Spark 9780228639022
Barnes & Noble 9780228639039
BWL Print 9780228639046

This book is a work of fiction, a product of the author's imagination. Any resemblance to actual events, people, or locations is coincidental and unintended.

## *Dedication*

To Kevin Grossheim - Voyageurs National Park Law Enforcement Ranger,

who died when his boat overturned while responding to a distress call.

## *Acknowledgements*

As always, my books are a collaboration, pulling ideas and information from many sources. I want to thank Osten Berg, who suggested much of the plot. Deanna Wilson read the roughest of rough drafts, corrected errors, grammar, punctuation, and inserted age-appropriate dialogue for some of my young characters (Who apparently use different jargon than I do). Garret Hovey and Fran Brozo guided me through the basics of cold-water scuba diving. Dan Fouts read an early draft and pointed out plot inconsistencies. Mike Westfall, Clem McIlravie, and Fran Brozo offered broad input on plot holes, dangling loose ends, and the overall book feel. Natalie Lund polices my overuse of prepositions and improves the readability of my prose. A final proofreading by Deanna Wilson and Anne Flagge catches the last random word fragments and typos. Any mistake sneaking past them is all on me. Many thanks to J.D. Shipton, Jude Pittman, and Susan Peters-Davis at BWL Publishing, who offer me endless support and turn my manuscripts into readable books.

*"Someone once said that when you die of hypothermia, you get cold and sleepy, things slow down, and then you just drift away."*
– Ottessa Moshfegh

# Table of Contents

# Chapter 1

We were finishing my mother-in-law's hearty ranch breakfast when my cell phone rang. Excusing myself from the table, I stepped outside to answer the call. "Hi, Jack," I said to my boss, the director of the US National Park Service Investigative Services Branch.

"Are you still in South Dakota, or back in Texas?"

"We celebrated my father-in-law's birthday yesterday in Spearfish. Our plan is to spend a few more days here, then fly back to Corpus Christi."

"I need to change that plan. Can you fly into International Falls from Spearfish?"

Trying to understand his request, I pictured northern Minnesota. "I doubt International Falls has a commercial airport. We would probably have to fly into Duluth or Minneapolis, then drive from there. What's going on? I don't recall any Park Service properties there."

"Your destination is Voyageurs National Park. The nearest town of any size is International Falls. I see another dot on the map that might be closer. It's Ely." (Jack pronounced it Eel-eye.)

Chuckling, I replied, "That's Ely, pronounced EEL-EE. The locals joke about identifying outside visitors and new weather forecasters based on whether they pronounce Ely correctly. They also call International Falls, *Frostbite Falls*. When I was a kid, the car manufacturers parked their vehicles on the lake and tried to start them when the temperature hit -30°."

"Thanks for the local perspective," Jack replied sarcastically. "I need you two at the park to help investigate an apparent murder."

"An *apparent* murder? You're not sure if the victim was killed?"

"That's something to be discussed with the medical examiner. The victim probably drowned some time ago." Jack paused, then said, "Both you and Jill have PADI scuba certifications noted in your files. Are they current?"

"Whew. I got my certification when I was in Boy Scouts. I dove a couple of times with the St. Paul Fire Department during drills, but I literally have not had a scuba tank strapped to my back for decades. Jill never mentioned scuba diving, so I assume her certification is also historical." I paused. "Are you hinting that this drowning investigation might involve scuba diving? Hasn't the body been recovered?"

"Not all of him has been recovered. A lower leg and foot were recovered. They were attached to a boat anchor. If not for the knotted rope around the ankle, this might've been investigated as an accidental drowning. The ME has tentatively ruled the death as suspicious. He's certain the victim was murdered."

I tried to picture the scene being described. "You said drowning, but only a lower leg and foot were discovered. Was the victim dismembered?"

"We believe the victim was probably intact when he died. Decomposition left only the skeleton."

"You must have more skilled divers than Jill and me who can search for the rest of the remains."

"That's in progress. I thought you might like to get a close-up look at the underwater scene."

I tipped my head back and clenched my eyes shut for a second, picturing a foot tied to an anchor. Then I stared at the horses grazing in the pasture. "In this case, I think underwater pictures of the scene and a visit to the ME will be sufficient."

"Karen Swift is the park superintendent. She's expecting your call. I told her you were a scuba diver, former Boy Scout, and proficient canoer."

"Jack, I think you've oversold my skill set."

"I've heard the park is beautiful. You're a Minnesotan, have you ever been there?"

"Yes, northern Minnesota is beautiful, and a lot of it is still wilderness. I've canoed the Boundary Waters Canoe Area, but I've never gone as far west as the national park."

"Please call Karen, then update me on your plans."

I was about to continue my protest when I realized he'd hung up. I leaned on the fence, hoping to come up with a great excuse for turning down an assignment that might involve canoes and/or scuba diving. Jill's cousin, Susie, was replacing shingles on the bunkhouse roof as the horses, unaccustomed to people in the old structure, watched suspiciously from the corral. Joker, a docile horse who'd befriended me during our Theodore Roosevelt National Park investigation, wandered over and nuzzled my hand as if expecting me to have an apple.

"Hi, guy. Sorry, no apples today and no trail ride either. Jill and I are off to Minnesota."

The sound of the persistent South Dakota wind covered Jill's approach. "We're off to Minnesota?" Jill leaned on the fence rail next to me, so our shoulders were touching.

"I didn't know you were scuba certified."

Jill cocked her head. "Where did that come from?"

"Jack called. He reviewed our files and saw we were both PADI scuba certified. He's assigned us to investigate an underwater murder scene."

"That certification was decades ago. I haven't had a tank on in...thirty years. I'm sure the technology is totally different." She paused, then asked, "How long ago were you certified?"

"When I was a Boy Scout, so before I turned eighteen."

"No, we're not taking a case that requires diving. We'd need to retake the training. I couldn't swim far enough to pass anymore."

"I already told Jack I would happily look at pictures of the underwater crime scene. He was undeterred."

"What and where?"

"A foot was found tied to an anchor in Voyageurs National Park."

"That's like almost in Canada, right?"

"As I recall, the international border is the northern edge of the park. The US/Canadian border runs down the center of Rainy Lake."

Jill's horse, Bill, having decided Susie was neither a threat nor a source of treats, walked over and nuzzled Jill's hand.

"Susie is putting a lot of effort into the bunkhouse. How long is she staying?"

Jill and I watched as Susie pried off some rotten cedar shingles and prepared to replace them. "Mom told Susie to stay as long as she needed. The job market for fifty-eight-year-old forest management specialists is tight."

"As long as she likes might be a long time."

"She's recently divorced, without a job, and has no job prospects. Nobody was using the bunkhouse, and she's not in Mom or Dad's way. I think her being here is okay."

"She's probably earning her keep by cleaning and fixing the bunkhouse," I observed. "I think Susie has OCD. She's tearing into the repairs like a woman obsessed."

Changing the topic, Jill asked, "What's the nearest airport to Voyageurs National Park?"

"The nearest town is International Falls. Duluth probably has the closest commercial airport. It's a couple of hours away from the park headquarters."

Jill took out her phone and punched in information. "Delta has daily flights from Minneapolis to International Falls."

"There you go! Call the travel office and book us on flights from Rapid City to Minneapolis, then to International Falls. I'll call the park superintendent and tell her we're on our way."

"With any luck, she'll say the murder has been solved, and we're not needed."

I petted Joker one last time. "And maybe we'll see a pig fly over the barn."

# Chapter 2

Karen Swift answered her phone on the first ring. "Superintendent Swift."

"This is Doug Fletcher from the Park Service Investigative Services Branch. I understand you're expecting my call."

"Hey, thanks for getting back to me. I've got my hands full with no way to deal with this...anchor murder."

"You're calling the case the anchor murder?"

"Actually, the local newspaper coined that phrase. It's caught on."

"I understand the bones were sent to a medical examiner?"

"Right, the ME in Duluth. There wasn't much to work with, just the lower leg and foot bones. Because of the knotted anchor rope he's treating the death as a homicide."

"Not a suicide?"

The pause was so long I began to wonder if we'd been disconnected. "Um...I can't get my head around the idea of tying an anchor to my own foot and jumping into the lake. I mean..."

"Let's assume this was a homicide. How would the victim get to the location where the body was found?"

"The body was recovered from Black Bay on Rainy Lake. To be honest, Rainy Lake is 360 square miles with connections to the entire Rainy River watershed. Voyageurs National Park also abuts the Boundary Waters Canoe Area, Superior National Forest, and Ontario's Quetico Provincial Park. The shoreline includes the cities of International Falls, Minnesota and Fort Frances, Ontario. There are literally a thousand places in Minnesota and Canada where a killer could've launched a boat, kayak, or canoe to deliver the body to where it was found."

"We just finished an investigation in Theodore Roosevelt National Park. It's 46,000 acres and I felt that was overwhelming."

"I'm sorry to sound negative, Fletcher. If I hadn't just entered this in the Park Service database as a possible murder, no one would've done anything except treat this as an oddity. That's how the sheriff's department is treating it. Believe me, there are plenty of oddities up here."

"We're flying into International Falls, probably tomorrow. What lodging would you suggest?"

"You're still planning to come up here?"

"My boss expects me to do an investigation. That's what we'll do."

"Okay, then. Let me make a couple of calls. There are some small resorts with guest cabins not far from where the body was found. They're not fancy, but they'll have clean sheets and an indoor bathroom."

I chuckled. "An indoor bathroom is always a plus."

"Everett Larson is one of my law enforcement rangers. Let me know when your flight will arrive. I'll have him pick you up."

"We can rent a car."

"We're talking about International Falls, not Chicago. If you could rent a car, you'd be lost most of the time you're here. The roads are poorly marked, GPS is as likely to deliver you to a swamp as your obscure destination, and not all of the locals are willing to give directions to a federal law enforcement officer. As a matter of fact, some of them would take great joy in sending you the wrong direction."

"Gee, that sounds lovely."

"Welcome to the boonies. People live here because they want to be off the grid. That attracts an interesting array of personalities, most of them belligerent and hostile to outsiders and people wearing badges."

"It's a national park. You get lots of outside visitors. The locals must want their business."

"It's a love/hate thing. The businesses would disappear without tourism. But the tourists bring in a lot of unwanted issues and often tend to treat the local folks as backwater hicks.”

“I think you just told me some of the locals *are* backwater hicks.”

“Yeah, well, the backwater hicks don’t want to be told they’re backwater hicks. Those hicks are about a fifty-fifty split of people trying to live off the land and others trying to escape the big city rat race who outnumber the locals for three months out of the year.”

“You make it sound like a really interesting place with a lot of culture clashes.”

Karen sighed. “Welcome to my world. A place where everyone feels the laws don’t apply. Let me know when your plane will arrive. Your escort will probably be happy to have someone sane to talk to for a while.”

“My partner, Jill, will be travelling with me.”

“Is your partner Jill Rickowski? I heard she had moved into law enforcement.”

“She’s Jill Fletcher now. We’re married.”

“No shit? Jill Rickowski is married? It’ll be fun to reconnect with her. We worked together in the Ozarks.”

“I’ll have Jill call you with our itinerary.”

I hunted Jill down and gave her the news about her former co-worker being the park superintendent and the area being full of belligerent people who think the laws don’t apply to them.

Our South Dakota departure was tear-filled and stressful. As we walked through the Rapid City airport, Jill bumped shoulders with me. "It's getting harder to leave."

"Our parents are getting older."

"I feel like I should be here for them."

"You could be their driver and medicalese interpreter."

"Us being there would make their lives easier."

"Maybe Susie can help with those issues, too," I suggested.

"Susie will leave as soon as she gets another job."

"As you pointed out, the job market for fired BLM employees is probably saturated. Maybe Susie will fill in as the South Dakota caregiver for a while."

Sighing, Jill agreed. "Maybe. It's just hard watching our parents aging while we're far away."

"Trust me, it would look worse in person."

There was no easy way to travel from Rapid City to International Falls. With a two-hour layover in Minneapolis, the trip took the whole day. Late in the afternoon, our pilot suggested looking out of the window. Below us, I saw the reason

Minnesota is called the land of 10,000 lakes. The landscape glistened like diamonds as the afternoon sun reflected off lakes and ponds as far as I could see.

Equally awestruck, Jill said, "It looks like God came through with a giant ice cream scoop and created all of those little lakes out of the forest."

Recalling my Minnesota grade school history, I said, "The legend of Paul Bunyan says the lakes are Babe the Blue Ox's footprints."

"I'd forgotten about Paul Bunyan."

"I think glaciers are a more likely cause of the lakes."

"That's what happened. The glaciers came through and scoured the land, scraping out potholes. When the glaciers melted, this region became a plain with water-filled potholes."

Jill pulled me close and whispered, "Like I said, God scooped out all of those lakes."

I kissed the top of Jill's head as the flight attendant walked past. She smiled at me, glanced at our intertwined hands, then at my badge. "I've never seen cops holding hands."

"She's afraid of flying. I'm trying to comfort her."

The flight attendant laughed when Jill rolled her eyes. "We'll be landing in a few minutes. Are you two lovebirds good for now?"

"Do you spend any time in International Falls?"

The flight attendant shook her head. "We're a Minneapolis-based crew. We just fly in and turn around unless there's a mechanical problem or weather."

I felt the landing gear deploy as the seat belt lights came on. We got a glimpse of Rainy Lake as the pilot made his final approach to the International Falls airport. The ragged shoreline extended as far as I could see, with dozens of bays and hundreds of islands.

We gathered our carry-ons and shuffled ahead as the passengers moved toward the exit. The pilot, previously informed of our firearms, stood in the cockpit door. He nodded for me to step aside.

"Thanks for keeping an eye on things in the back. I always appreciate having a law enforcement person aboard."

I swatted a pesky mosquito that landed on my neck. "I'd forgotten about the bugs."

Chuckling, the pilot said, "International Falls is literally the only airport that has us hold for ten minutes before taking off. We have to swat all of the mosquitoes in the cockpit before we pull onto the runway."

"You're kidding."

"Really. This time of year, they're the size of Piper Cubs and annoying as hell. The FAA doesn't want us to crash the plane because we're distracted." He swatted a mosquito that landed on his arm. "I hope you brought a supply of high DEET bug repellent if you plan to spend any time outside."

Jill stopped me as soon as we exited the jetway. "What did the pilot want?"

"He warned me about the mosquitoes."

"Great. Welcome to Minnesota, where the loon and mosquito are the state birds."

A young law enforcement ranger with sandy hair and striking blue eyes was waiting for us at the arrival gate. He nodded as we approached and extended his hand. "I'm Everett Larson. Welcome to I-Falls."

"Doug and Jill Fletcher. Nice to meet you."

He gestured away from the gate. "I assume you two have checked luggage."

"Two bags."

While waiting for the luggage to be unloaded, I asked, "What do you know about the body they found?"

"The fire department divers revisited the site a couple of times and have found a few more bones."

"The bones aren't all in the same area?" Jill asked.

"We think the ice moved them around."

"The ice? How deep is the water where the body was found?"

"I guess it's like ten feet deep."

Jill frowned. "And the bones were affected at that depth?"

Everett considered the question for a moment. "The ice is sometimes over six feet deep here. If that poor soul was still in one piece, his upper body would probably have been in solid ice, while his feet were anchored to the bottom. The ice moves around in the spring, so he probably got dragged a bit from wherever he went in."

I nodded. "And the next year, the ice might've only moved the upper part of him."

Everett nodded. "So, his torso, arms, and head might be a distance away from his feet."

Jill glanced around to make sure no one was listening to us. "Let's finish this conversation somewhere away from civilians."

Everett looked around. "I think I'm done."

The luggage arrived, and Everett led us to a Park Service pickup with law enforcement markings and a light bar. He lifted the bags into the pickup bed and unlocked the doors.

"How often are the divers searching?" I asked as I buckled in.

"They're fire department volunteers, so they're only available on the weekends. Because the water is still extremely cold, they wear neoprene wetsuits and only are down for twenty or thirty minutes a day." He paused, then added, "We've got people searching with underwater cameras, too. They can cover a lot more water."

"Where are we staying?"

"Karen booked you into Davidson's Resort. It looks like a nice place with a dozen cabins and a lodge that serves walleye sandwiches, burgers, and pizza."

I turned to Jill, smiling. "Yum. Fish, burgers and pizza."

Not realizing our distinctly different meal preferences, Everett added, "The rangers like to go to Davidson's because of their pizzas. I think they're handmade. Most of the other resorts bake frozen pizzas."

"Yum," Jill said, almost sounding sincere.

"Tell us more about the *modern* cabin we're renting. Modern, meaning it includes a bathroom."

Everett didn't have a poker face, so a smile flickered before he answered, "*Modern* cabins include an indoor bathroom. I hope Karen reserved a modern cabin for you. Most of the outhouses are creepy, especially at night." He glanced in the mirror, hoping to see Jill cringe.

"I grew up on a ranch that didn't have indoor plumbing until I was in fourth grade. I can deal with an outhouse. Doug on the other hand…"

"I can deal with an outhouse when required. I assume you're pulling our legs."

Everett seemed disappointed that we hadn't flinched at the possibility of an outhouse. "All of the resorts have indoor plumbing. The more upscale ones have hot tubs and spas."

"Are there a lot of secluded places where someone could've launched a boat to dump a body?"

"There are like a thousand places to launch a boat or canoe on Rainy Lake. Some are busier, like in I-Falls or at the bigger resorts. Others are private cabins, and canoe launches that see less activity. Realistically, no one would be surprised to see a fisherman show up with a tarp covering something."

"I suppose the victim might've been alive when they launched the boat. I don't suppose anyone would do a headcount on the number of people coming and going in each boat," I mused.

"Probably not," Everett replied. "Some of the resorts run a live camera feed 24/7. You can go online and see the weather any hour of the day, any day of the year. I don't know if they record the video."

Jill chuckled. "I wouldn't want to be the ranger assigned to watching ten years of 24/7 video feed from a dozen resorts."

Everett nodded his agreement. "You guys are assuming the victim was dumped in the summer. There are winter spear fishermen who cut holes large enough for someone to fall in."

"It's less likely they'd have an anchor handy," I replied.

We turned off the paved road onto a one-lane gravel driveway. A Davidson's Resort sign marked the turn.

"How far are we from the park headquarters?" Jill asked.

"We're a few miles from the Rainy Lake Visitor Center. The actual headquarters is in

International Falls, near the public boat launch. That's where all of the administrators are located."

"How large is the staff?" Jill asked.

"As you can imagine, there are a lot of seasonal employees in the summer and a ton of volunteers. There are about a dozen year-round administrators at the headquarters building. The park is 218,014 acres including 84,000 acres of water. Because of limited road access, there are visitor centers on Rainy Lake, Kabetogama, and Ash River. There's also a ranger station on Crane Lake."

"As a law enforcement ranger, what kind of problems do you deal with?"

"The usual stuff you find everywhere. There are drunks and people hunting illegally. There are unique problems like overloaded boats, people without life jackets, fishing law violations, people trying to bring motors to remote lakes restricted to canoes only, lost and injured hikers, boaters, and canoeists. It varies."

The narrow road, winding through the forest, opened into a parking area surrounded by cabins. A huge lodge with signs for food, groceries, bait, and fishing supplies was the centerpiece of the resort. Everett walked with us into the lodge to make sure we got checked in without a problem. He also carried our bags into our cozy cabin set back from Rainy Lake and fifty yards away from the resort boat launch.

Standing at the cabin door with the truck keys in hand, Everett swatted a mosquito on his neck and said, "I'll pick you guys up tomorrow morning. Are you early birds?"

"The lodge starts serving breakfast at six," I noted. "We'll probably miss the early fisherman rush and be eating by seven and ready to hit the road by eight, if that works for you."

"Sounds like a plan. I'll see you then."

# Chapter 3

After setting our bags inside the cabin, Jill and I walked around the collection of buildings that made up the outlying part of the resort. "This place looks like it went through ten-year evolutions." Jill observed as she swatted a mosquito on her arm. "I see tiny cabins originally built without kitchens or bathrooms that look like they were intended for serious fishermen. The clapboard siding set look like they were built when wives started coming along, requiring indoor plumbing and a small kitchen. The next evolution has cedar siding and appears to be large enough for a family or a party of six fishermen. The final evolution has siding intended to look rustic but are maintenance free. They have decks overlooking the lake, and I'll bet that alcove on the side has a hot tub."

The mosquitoes found us as we walked, a cloud of them circling our heads and landing on our arms, faces, and necks. I swatted the swarm with my Minnesota Twins cap, but it had little effect. We picked up the pace as we walked, hoping to outrun the pesky swarm.

Reaching the end of the driveway, we met four fishermen unloading groceries from a pickup towing a seriously large fishing boat on a double-axle trailer. From there, we turned around and walked to the lodge. "The lodge looks like it might be 1960s vintage," I observed. "I suppose the owners realized the value of having an on-site bait shop and restaurant."

"Being this far out of town, I imagine the fishermen didn't want to run back and forth to buy groceries or bait."

I laughed. "Or beer."

We paused on the lodge's top step to brush the mosquitoes off ourselves and to shoo the hovering swarm away from the door. The bar/restaurant was opposite the check-in desk. A hand-printed sign next to the entrance read SEAT YOURSELF. I spotted an open booth in the back and guided Jill past the high-top tables occupied by people drinking beer. The interior walls were knotty pine covered with mounted fish, deer heads, and pictures of the resort over the decades. Dozens of conversations bouncing off the wooden walls made it hard to hear the server when she came to take our drink order. According to the nametag pinned to her blue resort t-shirt, she was Megan. I assumed she was a local high school or college student working at the lodge for the summer.

Megan handed us laminated one-page menus and asked, "What can I get for you?" After noting our Diet Cokes on her order pad, she said, "Tonight's special is pan-fried walleye with fries and coleslaw." She left to get our beverages.

Jill looked at the menu, then nearly shouted to be heard over the noise. "The walleye sounds good."

I watched a male server pass carrying four orders of the walleye, the fillets hanging over the edges of the plates. "We could probably split one of those."

"I didn't think you liked freshwater fish."

"I was commenting on the volume more than my order preference."

Setting our drinks on the table, Megan asked, "Have you decided?"

Jill handed her the menu. "I'll try the pan-fried walleye special."

Megan nodded as she wrote, then she turned to me.

"I'd like a California burger."

"You get two sides. Would you like fries, slaw, or poutine?"

"Poutine?"

"It's fries and cheese curds with brown gravy. The Canadians love it."

Jill groaned.

"I'll have fries and slaw."

Jill scratched a red mosquito-bite welt on her arm as she leaned close. "Brown gravy over deep-fried cheese curds. Yuck."

I looked around the room, noting the smiling faces and fishermen's camaraderie. "If we weren't here to solve a murder, this would feel like a vacation."

Squirming, Jill scratched a mosquito bite on her shoulder. "Yeah, people hear about all of the places we've been and seem jealous of our travels. I don't argue with them, but the reality is we're in paradise and trying to figure out why someone died. That really takes away from the scenery." Rubbing the welt on her arm, she asked, "Didn't the mosquitoes get you?"

"I think I developed an immunity to them after camping with the Scouts."

"After supper, let's see if the grocery kiosk has insect repellent and itch relief balm."

I'd been casually watching the people coming and going through the front door. A couple stopped next to the seating sign at the door. The woman scanned the room as if looking for her party. Noting her gold badge on a gray uniform shirt, I said, "I think the woman who just walked in is a ranger."

Jill turned her head to see what had my attention. She slid out of the booth and waved. "Karen! Over here!"

Jill's friend was about our age with short, salt-and-pepper hair. She led a man who appeared to be old enough to be her father toward our table. The man's gray hair was cut short, and he wore a plaid shirt that strained against his substantial girth. Jill and Karen hugged as I stood.

"Jill, I don't think you've changed since I last saw you."

After their hug, Jill turned to me. "This is Karen Swift. Karen, this is my husband, Doug Fletcher."

Karen shook my hand and introduced Vic English. Jill slid into the booth next to me, sitting across from Karen and Vic. The more I looked at Vic, the more I thought *this guy is a cop.*

Reading my thoughts, Vic said, "I'm a retired I-Falls cop. Karen invited me along because I have a story that might interest you."

Our server swept over to the table and took Karen and Vic's orders for Lite beer. When she was gone, Vic leaned close. "I don't know exactly who your victim was, but I've got a good idea of when he went into the lake. I heard the ME is trying to recover enough DNA to attempt a match."

Vic stopped when Megan arrived with our beverages. "Have you guys made your menu selections?" Vic and Karen both ordered the pan-fried walleye. Megan assured us that she'd make sure all four meals came out at the same time.

Vic waited until Megan was gone, then leaned close again. "Years ago, I responded to a call about a blood trail coming out of The Bayside Motel. It's a sleazy joint that caters to seasonal workers who rent by the month.

A lot of the clientele are semi-indigents who work menial jobs around town during the tourist season. We always got calls from the motel about fights, noisy parties, and drug use." Vic paused to see if anyone was listening. "The manager came in one day and freaked out because there was a dribble of blood coming out of the front door and onto the sidewalk. He wasn't sure if it was coming or going, so he called 911. I took the call and talked to the manager/owner and the night manager, a bozo who apparently slept at the desk unless someone rang the bell. The night manager didn't know shit about the blood or even if anyone had arrived or left during the night."

Vic paused when Megan checked on our drinks and said our meals would be out in a few minutes.

"So, the manager and I follow the blood trail up the stairs. By then, half a dozen people have been up and down the stairs, and it's impossible to tell if one set of footprints is from a person who's carrying or dragging a body or if they're from the residents. We follow the blood to a motel room. I pound on the door and announce myself. There's no response, so the manager unlocks the door." Vic looked around, then went on. "The room looked like a slaughterhouse. Someone had tried to sop up blood on the floor with the sheets. Then, they'd thrown them into a bathtub full of water. There's blood splatter all over the place, and what appears to be arterial bleeding was squirted on the wall over one of the beds. I backed out of the room and told the manager to keep the door locked until investigators showed up. After I called it in, I followed the blood trail down the street for two blocks. It ended at the city boat launch, where someone apparently dumped the body into a boat and took it away."

"When did that happen?" I asked.

"June of '89. Almost forty years ago."

Two servers arrived with our meals and left. Vic popped a fry into his mouth and cocked his head. "Do you want me to go on, or would you rather wait until after we've eaten?"

Jill shrugged. "Since I've been partnered with Doug, I've become accustomed to hearing grisly crime scene details over meals."

Karen studied her walleye for a moment. "Let's talk about...the weather. How about those Twins? They're really off to a hot start, aren't they?"

Vic chuckled and dove into his walleye with gusto. Karen took a bite, then asked Jill, "When did you two get married? The last time I heard about you, there'd been an incident with hikers lost in a flash flood. Somehow, the powers that be felt you were responsible for that act of God."

"Doug and I investigated that flash flood incident together. After the investigation, it became clear I wasn't going to be the superintendent any longer. Doug invited me to join him at his new post in Texas until my Park Service position was sorted out, and one thing led to another." Jill paused, then asked, "You're still single?"

Karen nodded. "As you know, being a park superintendent doesn't lend itself to long-term relationships. You can't fraternize with your employees, and you only stay at the same park a few years. I dated some but never found that special someone who was interested in being with a Park Service vagabond."

I looked at Vic, thinking maybe they were dating. He shook his head and chuckled. "Karen and I are coffee buddies. I hang out at the café with a bunch of local retirees and Karen sometimes comes in for breakfast. I saw her in uniform one morning, so I went over to talk. You know how that goes. The fraternity of badges."

Karen whispered something to Jill while Vic was talking. Jill looked at me, grinned, then whispered back.

When it became clear the women weren't sharing their secret, I asked Vic, "How long were you an I-Falls cop?"

"They hired me right after I got out of the Navy. I retired thirty years later."

I nodded. "I imagine it's crazy here all summer and dead all winter."

Vic waved his fork as he spoke, "It's the dumbest damned thing. The bars are busiest on the coldest damn nights of the year. The temperature goes down, and people feel compelled to go out. I've had more DUI arrests in January than in any other month of the year. Oh yeah, then there are the ice fishermen. I swear, the only reason people ice fish is to get away from their wives while they drink. We sometimes set up a sobriety checkpoint at the boat launch. I swear to God we've arrested every other driver coming off the lake for either a DUI or an open bottle every January."

Jill and Karen talked about all of the different parks they'd worked in, then about all of the interesting investigations we'd been assigned. Once Megan verified that we were full and didn't want dessert, Vic leaned close again. "There was a marina full of boats, and I walked around, looking for one with blood on the transom. Nothing. I talked to the night walleye fishermen who were coming in off the lake, and nobody recalled seeing a body being loaded into a boat. I canvassed all of the businesses in town, but of course, no one was open in the middle of the night to see a body being dragged through downtown. This was back in the day before everyone had a camera on their doorbell, so there was no video."

"So, you never found out who the victim was or what happened to him?"

"The motel manager gave me the names of the two guys who'd rented the room. Both names were bogus. They'd paid by the week, in cash, so there was no credit card to trace.

My eyewitnesses said they'd been driving an old blue, green, or black pickup, that was either a Dodge, Ford, or Chevy."

I chuckled. "Don't you love getting eyewitness statements?"

Vic rolled his eyes. "So, I've got nothing but a blood trail and a room that looks like someone was killed in it."

"You're convinced the victim was dead?" Jill asked.

"Oh, yeah. With arterial blood splatter on the walls, I'm one hundred percent sure that victim was dead. There must've been a gallon of blood on the walls and sheets in the bathtub. Yeah, that guy's a goner."

The color drained from Karen's face as Vic told the story. She pushed her plate away and placed her napkin on top of the remaining walleye. Anxious to change the topic, she said, "I've got two fire department volunteer divers going down tomorrow morning at ten. Would you two like to dive with them?"

"No," I replied. "Neither of us has had scuba gear on for a long time and we didn't bring wetsuits. I think we'll talk to the divers when they come ashore."

"There's a lot of area to be covered. It'd be very helpful to have two more people helping with the search." Seeing our lack of enthusiasm, Karen added, "One of the I-Falls firemen is a certified divemaster who goes out with tourists. She could give you a refresher."

"What's the water like?" I asked, hoping that the conditions would prevent us from diving.

Vic responded first. Smiling, he said, "The ice has been off the lake for a couple of weeks, so the water is slightly above freezing."

Karen glared at him. "It's actually great diving right now. Yes, the water is cold, but it's clear. You can cover a lot of area on one air tank." Seeing Jill wavering, Karen added, "I'd really appreciate your help. We really need to find the rest of the skeleton. And you are both certified divers. There aren't many people around here who can dive."

"How deep are you searching?" I asked, remembering that a dive of thirty feet for any length of time was on the cusp of needing decompression time.

"The body was found in a shallow part of Black Bay. No one has been deeper than twenty feet." Karen looked at Vic. "That's right, isn't it?"

"I think the divers are focusing on the shallower areas, assuming the shifting ice probably pulled the torso toward shore. The ice was so thick the fishermen couldn't drill holes through to the water, even with extensions on their augers. I'm sure at least the guy's head was probably frozen solid in the ice." Vic chuckled. "Hitting that with your auger would sure ruin your day!"

Karen was staring at her plate with her hands flat on the table. I wondered how close she was to making a run to the bathroom. I put my hand on one of hers and said, "Take deep breaths and blow them out slowly. We're done talking about the murder, okay?"

Karen looked up and swallowed. "Yeah, um, give me a second." We stared at her silently. Then she slid out of the booth. "I'm going to splash cold water on my face."

Vic watched Karen walk away. He turned back to us. "I forget that she's a civilian wearing a uniform. I should probably watch what I say."

"You and Karen aren't an item?" Jill asked.

"Naw. We've had a couple of laughs together. I guess she doesn't have many people she can talk to about work things. I'm a good listener."

"How many times have you been divorced?" I asked.

Vic's grin was recognition that I knew exactly how hard a cop's job was on marriages. "Just twice...so far."

"That's gotta be tough in a small town," Jill suggested.

"I bump into my exes buying groceries or hardware. One of them works in the pharmacy. We've pretty much put our past behind us. It was a painful time, and now it's over. We're civil to each other."

"Is Karen a candidate for number three?" I asked.

Vic shrugged. "She's a nice kid. I'm not sure she's ready for cop stories and dealing with my PTSD. Most women aren't. It takes someone special to handle that, doesn't it Jill?"

With a mouthful of walleye, the question caught Jill by surprise. She glanced at me as she swallowed and wiped her mouth. "The pluses outweigh the minuses."

Vic smiled at me. "You found a keeper."

Karen returned to the table just in time to catch Vic's last comment. "Who's a keeper?"

"Jill," Vic replied. "She's figured out how to live with a cop."

Karen rolled her eyes. "That sounds like a line from a black and white movie. I think we've moved past women being *keepers,* or not."

Vic sighed and gave me a pleading look. "I missed the last diversity class before I retired."

I tried to move us back to the case. "Vic, did you check boats anywhere other than in the marina by town?"

Gesturing toward the windows overlooking the lake, Vic replied, "There were probably twenty thousand boats on the lake on any summer weekend. Half of them were in Canada. So, no, I didn't check anywhere except the marina in town."

Trying to tone down Vic's sharp response, Karen asked if we'd brought warm coats. "There's a cold front moving in. We might get snow flurries."

I grimaced. "Snow in June? Really?"

"The only month I-Falls hasn't had snow is August," Vic replied. "And we're not sure about August. The weather reporting station is at the airport. There are fishing guides who swear there were snowflakes in the air on August 20 in '67."

"We brought sweatshirts and windbreakers," Jill replied. "My winter gear is in South Dakota."

"I've got a couple of spare coats, stocking caps, and gloves." Karen sized me up. "They'll probably be snug on Doug and baggy on Jill."

"Doug, if you're willing to pin your badge on an I-Falls police coat, I can fix you up."

"That'd be great, Vic. Unless that would make me a target for some reason."

"This isn't Minneapolis. The locals still wave at cops when we drive past and buy us coffee when they see us in town."

Karen signaled for Megan to bring her the check. "Supper is on me tonight."

On the lodge's front steps, we shook hands with Vic and hugged Karen. "Everett is at your disposal for as long as you're here. If you need anything, let him know."

Vic leaned against my shoulder as we shook hands and whispered, "I've still got contacts in town. If you need anything from the city or county cops, let me know. I can make some calls."

After they drove away, Jill asked, "What are you thinking?"

"Vic is a sexist dinosaur. I'm disappointed with his follow-up on the blood trail. I assume there was some investigator assigned to the case who took it further."

"Wouldn't it be interesting if the assigned investigator was a woman? Vic would've discounted whatever she did."

"Let's not jump to conclusions." I reflected on Jill and Karen's conversation while Vic and I discussed the case. "What conspiracy were you and Karen whispering about?"

Jill smirked and took my hand. "Karen said you are ruggedly handsome. She thinks I'm very lucky to have met you."

"Her opinion may have changed when she turned green while we discussed the murder." I nodded toward the check-in desk in the lobby. "Let's see if the owners are around."

We showed our badges to the young woman at the desk and told her we wanted to introduce ourselves to the owner. She darted off. When the desk clerk returned, she asked us to take a seat near the fireplace.

Pine logs sparked in the fieldstone fireplace as we waited. A middle-aged, slender man with a nearly bald head showed up behind the desk. The desk clerk gestured toward us, and he approached, smiling. "I understand you're law enforcement folks. Welcome to the resort. I'm Max Davidson."

After introducing ourselves, we sat down with Davidson in front of the fireplace.

"We're investigating the anchor murder. I was hoping you could provide us with a historical perspective."

Davidson continued to smile. "Let me give you some history. My family has owned this resort for seventy years. I grew up here and was guiding fishermen on the lake when I was fourteen. What history would you like to know?"

"We spoke with Vic English about a murder downtown. He suspects the victim of that murder is the person whose foot was found tied to the anchor."

"I guess that's possible. What can I tell you that Vic didn't say?"

"Vic checked for blood in the boats parked at the marina in town. How would we find out if there was a bloody boat somewhere else?"

Davidson blew out a breath and leaned back. "Wow, that really is ancient history. When was that murder in town?"

"June 1989."

"I have a vague memory of rumors about that. I was only a teenager."

"Is there someone who'd remember that history?" Jill asked. "Your parents ran the resort back then. Do they still live locally?"

Max snorted. "They sold the resort to me and moved to Phoenix the next day. I could give you their phone number, but my dad's got a bit of dementia. He remembers some things clearly. Other times, he doesn't remember who I am." Davidson paused, deep in thought. "You need to talk to Karl Peterson. He's an old coot who lives next door. He's the local historian and storyteller."

"He lives next door? Is his place within walking distance?"

Davidson leaned onto his left hip and pulled out his cell phone. He selected a number from the phone's directory and let it ring. "Hey, Karl. It's Max Davidson. I've got a couple here who are interested in talking about that murder in I-Falls back in '89. Have you got a minute to spend with them?" He listened and nodded. "If you think a shot of blackberry brandy would help your memory, come on over. I'll pour it myself."

"Do you bribe him with blackberry brandy very often?" I asked as Davidson returned the phone to his pocket.

"If I get a bunch of discouraged fishermen in here who are too cheap to hire a guide, I invite Karl over. He unrolls a lake map and points out the hot spots for successful fishing at the prevailing water temperature and weather conditions as he drinks shots of blackberry brandy."

"And that works?"

"Sometimes. If nothing else, they get to hear the old man regale them with stories about stringers of fish so long they almost sank his boat, moose hunts that nearly killed him, and life in the old-time logging camps when it was so cold your spit froze before it hit the ground."

"He sounds colorful," Jill suggested. "Like my dad and Uncle Chet. You get a couple of shots of bourbon into them and ask a question about the old days. Then, all you do is sit back and listen."

I grimaced. "I never know how many of their tales are true or pure fiction."

"There's always a thread of truth in there."

"I think their stories improve with each telling. The snow was deeper, the shots were longer, the cattle were wilder, and they were young and handsome."

The lodge's front door opened, and a hulking old man well over six feet tall wearing a plaid flannel shirt and denim bib overalls walked in. He surveyed the room until Davidson stood. The man's eyes lit up, and he marched over to us. "Karl, these people are Doug and Jill, who are investigating the foot and anchor that were found in Black Bay."

Peterson pumped our hands, his massive hands engulfing ours. His smile revealed alternating teeth and empty gums. His shaggy white beard was speckled with bits of Copenhagen snuff. An aura of Old Spice aftershave, cooked cabbage, and body odor assaulted my nose as Max made the introductions.

"What can I tell you?" Karl asked.

Davidson gestured toward a hallway behind the front desk. "Let's move this discussion to my office. I think there's a bottle of blackberry brandy in my bottom desk drawer.”

Karl had shuffled in. After the mention of brandy, his gait sped up, and he led us to Davidson’s office as if on a mission. Karl sat in a chair to the side of the desk. Jill and I sat on a couch across from the desk. After pulling out the blackberry brandy, Max retrieved four glasses from a bar built into the wood-paneled wall.

“None for me,” I said before he poured.

“Not a fan of blackberry brandy?” Karl asked. “You apparently don’t know it has medicinal properties.”

“I’m not in need of medication right now, thanks.”

Max poured *two fingers* of the purple liquid into three glasses. He handed one to Karl, then rolled his chair around the desk so he was next to Jill. Max handed her a glass as Karl lifted his glass in a toast. “To history.”

After drinking half of his brandy in one swallow, Karl smacked his lips. Jill took a sip and started coughing. “This burns like it’s one-hundred proof.”

Max nodded. “The distributor gets it directly from Poland.”

“What do you need to know?” Karl asked after he downed the rest of his brandy and handed the glass back to Max for a refill.

“We understand there was a possible murder in town back in June of ’89. The body was dragged to the lake, but the cops never identified the victim, the killer, or the boat that removed the body. We suspect the foot tied to the anchor may be that murder victim."

Karl took his refilled glass and held it in both hands. He wrinkled his nose, which made his entire gray beard twitch. "As I recall, there wasn't a lot of effort put into that investigation."

When Karl paused to take another swallow of liquor, I asked, "Why would you think there wasn't much effort put into the investigation?"

"The guy who was killed was probably trash. Nobody knew him, and nobody cared that he might've been killed. The motel didn't have his right name, so everyone figured he was mixed up in that meth ring that was working here about then. I think the cops were relieved that a couple of those jerks were gone."

"There was a methamphetamine ring operating here?" I asked.

"Weren't they pretty much everywhere back then?"

"You don't know who they were? Did you hear any rumors?"

"I never heard any names. I just know they'd been staying at the motel while their buddies were cooking meth at a house somewhere in the woods."

"I wouldn't expect meth dealers to have a boat," I opined.

Karl shook his head. "I'm sure they stole one if they needed it."

"We should check with the cops to see if any boats were reported stolen."

"Don't need to," Karl replied as he held out his glass for another refill.

"Why not?" I asked as Davidson smiled at me. He poured another two fingers of brandy into Karl's glass.

"We found Randy Mischke's boat washed up on shore a day later." Karl nodded toward our host. "Max and his dad found it on this side of the bay. His motor and gas tank were still in it, so he never called the sheriff."

"Do you know if it was smeared with blood?" Jill asked.

"It wouldn't have been. It got loose during the storm. It was half full of rainwater when they found it. Randy was the only one who was convinced it had been stolen. But he drinks a lot and probably wasn't sober enough to remember if he'd even tied it up after he'd been out night fishing."

"Does Randy still live around here?" I asked.

Davidson nodded, "He's in the last house out on Rocky Point. He's got a light on the end of his dock that's kind of a local beacon."

"Thanks," I said as I stood and patted Karl on the shoulder.

Karl cocked his head. "Don't you want to know why Randy was sure his boat had been stolen?"

"Sure. Why did he think that?" I asked.

"His anchor was gone. Boats that blow away don't lose their anchors. I've heard Randy say a hundred times that someday he was going to find the sonofabitch who stole his anchor."

"How will he know it's his anchor and not someone else's?"

Karl swilled the last of his liquor and stood. "Randy's a welder. He fixes all kinds of stuff for people. He welds his initials on all of his own stuff. RM."

After escorting Karl to the door and handing him the rest of the brandy, Davidson turned to us. "I hope that's a useful lead."

"It's certainly worth a follow-up," I replied. "I think we owe you a couple bottles of Polish brandy."

Max chuckled and shook his head. "I buy it by the case to stay on Karl's good side. The tourists enjoy having him come around to provide local color. We all come out ahead."

Jill leaned close to me as we walked to our cabin, making sure no one was around. "Karl had old man smell."

"Huh?"

"Uncle Chet used to have it before your mom moved in with him. You know, kind of like unwashed socks soaked in cooked cabbage. I think he spritzed some Old Spice to cover it all."

"Chet used to be like that?"

"I think you get used to the background smell when you live alone in it. Your mom opens the windows and makes Chet bathe."

"Cooked cabbage?"

"Chet lived on cabbage fried in lard. Cabbage doesn't spoil, is cheap, and frying it takes no talent at all." Jill paused as we walked. "I'm sure that's why Chet ate at our house all of the time. He got some variety."

"And company. Chet is very social."

# Chapter 4

Law Enforcement Ranger Everett Larson walked into the resort's restaurant promptly at 8:00 a.m. Since we were two of only six people at that hour of the morning, he had no problem spotting us. He waved at the young waitress standing behind the bar, who responded by pouring him a cup of coffee. He nodded his thanks as she delivered it to our booth. He said, "You've got the early shift, Laney. I probably should've brought you home earlier."

The young woman smiled at Larson as she added coffee to Jill and my cups. "It's okay, Ev, I wasn't in a hurry to get home. I'll probably take a nap after the noon rush."

Feeling like he'd missed a social obligation, Everett shifted his focus from the cute young woman to us. "Sorry. I should've introduced you to Laney. We're dating."

"I caught that," Jill replied, smiling.

Laney glanced at the other diners to make sure no one needed anything, then she turned to Jill. "I'm from Shakopee and a student at Minnesota State Mankato, just working here for the summer. I met Ev the first week I was at the resort."

"Mankato to International Falls is one heck of a long-distance relationship," I joked as I set the napkin on my breakfast plate.

Laney drew a sharp breath. "I've got a boyfriend in Mankato. Ev and I are just having a good time. Nothing serious, right, Ev?"

"I guess we'll see if I can sway your feelings over the next two months."

The topic must've been uncomfortable because Laney needed to check on something in the kitchen, then fled. Everett watched as she walked away.

"Is Laney someone special?" Jill asked.

"I kinda hope she'll become that. She's different from the local girls. It seems that half of them get engaged by the time they graduate from high school. The other half are hoping to marry an up-and-coming hockey star, or they move to the Twin Cities to get a 'real' job."

"Do many of the girls marry hockey stars?" Jill asked.

"Naw. That doesn't stop them from trying. They're all hoping to hook up with the next Wayne Gretzky. Most of that group end up with broken hearts while drowning their sorrows at the local watering holes." Everett paused for a second, then added, "I tried that scene. Most of them freak out when they find out I'm a cop."

Laney returned from the kitchen carrying a small plate with a scoop of cherry pie filling sprinkled with pie crust. She set it in front of Everett and produced a fork from her apron, then smiled at him. "Here you go. I can never get the first slice of pie to look good enough to serve to a paying customer."

"Thanks!" he replied as he dove into the pie.

"What time are you picking me up tonight?"

Nodding to us, he said, "It depends on when I finish up with the Fletchers."

Laney looked at me and raised her eyebrows with an unasked question.

"I don't think we'll have anything that'll require your attention past five o'clock. Unless something unforeseen comes up, Everett should be free any time after that."

"Since I'm dropping them off here, I could pick you up at the same time. We can go back to my place and bake a pizza while I change out of my uniform."

Laney's eyes lit up. "We can binge season eight of 'Supernatural.'"

After that announcement, Laney was summoned by a customer who wanted to pay their bill.

"'Supernatural?'" Jill asked.

"We've been working our way through all the thrillers on Netflix." Everett leaned close and whispered, "I'm more into thrillers and cop shows, but Laney really likes the spooky shows."

"The things we do for love," I said as I stood.

"What would you like to do today?" Everett asked as we walked to the pickup.

"We'd like to talk to the divers who are searching the lake," I replied. "There's also a welder whose boat was stolen about the same time as the guy who disappeared from the motel. I'd like to talk to Randy Mischke."

"I don't know anything about someone disappearing from a motel."

"Vic English stopped by during supper and told us about his investigation into an apparent murder in the motel. He said it was a bloody mess, but he never found the body."

Everett grimaced at the mention of Vic English.

"Do you have a problem with Vic?"

"He schmoozes anyone wearing a badge as if we're his old friends. He's always asking about our cases and trying to dig into confidential stuff."

"I think that happens to a lot of retired cops. They either walk away and never look back, or they never let go."

"Let's go to the fire station," Everett suggested. "We can probably catch the divers while they load their gear."

* * *

As predicted, three cars were parked at the fire station. We found two men and a woman inside wearing blue fire department uniforms checking air tanks. They all looked up when we opened the door.

"Hey, guys," Everett said as we stepped in. "This is Doug and Jill Fletcher. They're Park Service investigators from Texas."

The three divers looked at each other, frowning. "Texas?" The woman stepped forward and offered her hand. "I'm Rachel Murphy. My two partners are Lance and Parker." Rachel appeared to be about forty with a touch of gray in her short brown hair.

"Nice to meet you. We'd like to pick your brains about the water conditions and what you're finding."

Lance cocked his head. "You're coming along, aren't you? We heard you two were PADI certified divers."

Jill snorted. "Our diving credentials may have been oversold. Doug and I *were* both dive certified. However, neither of us has had a scuba tank on in years. If you need us to dive, you may have to give us a refresher."

"Did you bring your PADI cards?" Rachel asked.

Smiling, I said, "No cards. I guess we can't dive with you."

Rachel stepped to a desktop computer in the corner. "All the PADI certifications are online. Give me a second to pull yours up." She glanced at Jill and asked, "Did you certify in Texas? Warm water ocean dives?"

"It'll be under Jill Rickowski. I was certified in the Ozarks. Most of my experience was diving in the manmade lakes in Missouri. It wasn't really warm water diving. When the water gets warm, algae blooms, and it's impossible to see anything."

"Here's Jill. You're good to go. How about you, Doug, where were you certified?"

"I dove with the Boy Scouts," I explained. "We used Square Lake, near Stillwater, for our open water dive. It's spring-fed, deep, and cool."

Rachel typed into the computer and waited. "Yup, here you are, Doug. Certification in 1988."

Lance said, "Jill, this is going to be like having someone pour ice water down your shirt. We wear wetsuits and the first jolt of cold fades as the water inside of the neoprene warms up. The lake water is literally only a few degrees above freezing this time of year. It's closer to a polar plunge than it is to jumping into an Arkansas lake. Are you sure you want to do this?"

I could almost feel Jill's steely resolve. She didn't like having men tell her she wasn't capable of doing something. I tried to stop her but was a beat too late. "That sounds invigorating. Can you guys lend us wetsuits, familiarize us with your gear, then lead us through the dive?"

Lance's smirk was priceless. "I'd love to." He looked at Everett. "Are you diving too?"

"I've never done anything but snorkel in the Bahamas. I don't even like wading in Rainy Lake."

Lance led us into a changing room where he opened a locker filled with black wetsuits.

He pulled out two of them and returned, handing one to Jill. "The women's room is by the office." As Jill walked away, he handed one to me. "Are you serious about this? The water is bone chilling cold."

I patted my stomach. "I've got some built-in insulation. Jill will have to rely on the wetsuit to keep her warm."

"You two really don't have to do this. It'll take us a couple of weeks to grid search the east side of Black Bay, but we'll get through it."

"My partner..."

Lance smiled. "Your partner bristled when I told her she couldn't do it. She's feisty, isn't she?"

"She doesn't react well to being told no or having something mansplained to her."

"Is Jill your boss?"

"We're partners. Although she's got more years with the Park Service, I've got more years in law enforcement."

"You two are married, right?"

"Right."

"You must have some knock-down battles."

I shrugged. "Don't all married couples have their moments?"

"Not many couples carry guns."

"Don't worry, we won't shoot each other, or you."

The firemen loaned us heavy "bunker" coats to wear over our wetsuits during our drive to the boat launch. We placed our firearms in Everett's care, then rode with him to the boat landing. "I've got to say, you two are either crazy or seriously impaired. That water is ice cold, and those bones have been missing for a long time. What's to gain from finding another piece of the dead guy?"

"If we locate his head, a forensic odontologist might be able to identify the victim, and his pelvis might be the best hope for recovering DNA."

Reading Everett's skepticism, Jill added, "The victim has a family who are wondering where he or she is. We might be able to give them closure."

"And possibly link him to his killer," I added. "Most murder victims are known to their assailant."

"I've seen the people coming and going from that motel. Their families probably gave up on those losers a long time ago. Each of them looks like they've got a lifetime of bad choices behind them. That kind of history doesn't endear you to spouses, parents, or siblings."

I chuckled and replied, "We just wrapped up a case in Kentucky. The detective we worked with located a girl who'd been lured away by a pimp. Kristina found the girl and returned her to her parents. The parents were delighted, even though their daughter had been through two years of hell with the pimp. Yes, there's some healing that's got to happen, but that result makes all the effort worthwhile."

"Do you think this victim might've been a missing teen?"

"We won't know until we identify him or her."

The firemen launched their boat while we sat in the warm Park Service pickup. Once the boat was tied up, they started loading gear into it. I looked at Jill. "Showtime."

Jill trudged to the dock. "I can't believe I let those guys bait me into doing this."

"We could back out."

Jill sighed. "No. We're doing this. If nothing else, just so we can tell Jack we made every effort to identify the victim."

Once we were in the boat, Rachel trained us on the use of scuba gear and the floatation vest. "Since we'll be in less than thirty feet of water, you don't need to decompress. Just swim to the surface and remember to exhale as you ascend."

The basic gear hadn't changed since I'd been certified. We wore neoprene gloves and booties. The tank was heavy as I strapped it to my back, and the mask was tight on my face. Lance checked my gear as the boat slowed. "Take a couple of breaths from the regulator before we go in." I followed his directions and gave him a thumbs up.

Rachel tapped my shoulder and shouted so I could hear through the Neoprene hoodie and over the sound of the outboard. "Never let your partner out of your sight. The visibility is good, so you can separate a few feet and still stay in contact. We'll drop you and Lance off here. Jill and I will start our search about one hundred yards farther down. Stay safe."

After putting on our swim fins, Lance stepped over the gunwale onto the top step of a ladder, then let go, flopping backwards into the water. I tried to mimic his move, but the swim fins made movement cumbersome, and I lost my grip before I had my second foot on the ladder. In less than a second, I was blinded by the bubbles I'd created as I splashed into the water. My face felt stung by tiny ice crystals, and cold water seeped into the wetsuit around my neck, ankles, and wrists. Even before I was fully oriented, Lance put his hand on my arm, making sure I knew he was there and checking that my regulator was working properly.

I nodded, then he raised his hand out of the water to signal we were okay. A small splash followed as someone in the boat tossed out a buoy with a red flag and white diagonal line to signal other boaters that there were divers in the area. The boat drifted a few yards away, then the propeller spun as they sped off. For a second, I had the chilling feeling that I was going to be left to die.

Lance patted my arm, then pointed to the bottom, which seemed only ten feet away. Through a series of hand signals, he indicated the direction we were going to travel and that he was moving a few feet away from me. He pointed at my eyes, then at him, reminding me to keep him in sight.

The whine of the boat's motor diminished as they sped away. The bubbles coming from my regulator were the only sound. In a moment of panic, I started breathing too fast, then I reminded myself that I was safe and focused on breathing regularly.

I watched Lance swim a few feet before he turned to look at me. The water was so clear I could see the bottom twenty feet past him. After a hand signal to move in the direction the boat had gone, I kicked and started gliding through the water. Within a few yards, I'd checked Lance's position twice and stared at a large walleye who was laying inert on the bottom until I spooked him.

I quickly got into the rhythm of visually searching the area around me, then checking Lance's position. Time sped by as we moved across the bottom. I noticed him checking his dive watch, which reassured me he was monitoring our time on the bottom. I checked the pressure regulator, reassuring myself the needle was still well into the green, safe portion of the dial.

After a few minutes, Lance signaled for me to stop and swim to him. I checked my air supply, which was still well into the green. Slightly confused about his intentions, I swam to him as he hovered. When I reached him, he pointed at the bottom. I saw something white, hardly larger than a silver dollar. Lance flipped over and swam down to the bottom. Fluttering his hands, he caused eddies of silt. As they drifted away, I saw the shaft of a bone. Once he was sure I understood what we were seeing, he reached down and pulled it loose from the silt. Not being a doctor, but having seen a lot of autopsies and trauma, I realized he'd uncovered one of the lower human arm bones, a radius or ulna.

He slipped the bone into a mesh bag, then swung his hands to uncover more of the area around the bone. Catching on to his plan, I turned the opposite direction and mimicked his motion. After a few looks to make sure Lance was still in sight, I swirled away the silt on another section of the bottom, exposing a small white bone.

When Lance looked up, I signaled him that I'd found something. As he swam over, I fanned my hand back and forth over the area, causing a silt cloud obscuring my view of the bottom. It started to clear as Lance approached. We hovered over the spot for another minute waiting for the water to clear. Lance lifted his gauge and held up five fingers, which I assume meant we had five minutes before we needed to surface.

Something gold flickered on the bottom as passing waves filtered the sunlight. Around the glimmering gold, tiny white bones appeared. I gestured for Lance to retrieve the scattered bones. He shook his head and made a gracious gesture, indicating it was my find to retrieve.

My fins stirred up the silt again when I flipped over. As I reached out for the gold ring that shimmered beneath me, I realized there was still a small finger bone running through it. I hesitated, waiting for the silt to clear. In a few moments, the finger bones, and other bones of the hand/wrist appeared through the silty water. I looked at Lance, who gestured for me to put them into my bag. My fingers seemed like sausages that didn't want to flex or clamp onto the tiny bones. My first thought was that the neoprene gloves were limiting my flexibility. I soon realized the problem was with my cold fingers that could barely sense when I'd grasped a tiny bone. The whine of an approaching boat motor traveled through the water, slowing at it neared us.

I'd retrieved about a dozen small bones when Lance tapped my arm and signaled for us to ascend. After a quick check for more bones, I nodded and followed him to the surface.

With the motor off, the boat bobbed above us, slowly drifting with the waves. Lance gestured for me to climb the ladder first, then followed. Once in the boat, he pulled off his mask. "Mark this GPS location! We found a hand and an arm bone."

Parker, the fireman operating the boat nodded and punched a button on the GPS monitor. "It's in the log."

Parker helped me take off the scuba tank. He secured it in a rack, then pulled a gallon thermos out of a storage compartment. He handed me a steaming cup.

"Coffee?" I slurred, realizing that my lips were so cold I couldn't form words.

"Hot chocolate. It warms you from the inside and provides a few calories."

The liquid seemed to burn my lips, and I recoiled.

"It's okay," Parker reassured me as he poured a cup for Lance. "It just seems really hot because your lips are so cold."

I took another sip, savoring the sweet warmth before swallowing. "I thought you'd have a bottle of brandy," I quipped. "We were recently in Kentucky. The locals talked about the Kentucky hug, the warmth you feel when you take a sip of bourbon."

Lance shook his head. "Alcohol is a vasodilator. That's the worst thing you could drink right now. We want to warm our cores first. If you take a drink of brandy, it'll open your peripheral blood vessels and send a shock wave of cold to your heart. We've had a few hypothermia cases among ice fishermen who'd been chugging schnapps or Canadian whiskey. Alcohol can be a killer when you're hypothermic."

I was startled when a black neoprene hoodie appeared over the gunwale. A second later, Jill's head and torso appeared, and she climbed into the boat. After stepping aside to allow Rachel space to climb aboard, Jill pulled out her mouthpiece and removed her mask. Her lips were blue, and her shivering hand reached for my cup. "I AM F-F-F-FROZEN."

Parker poured two more mugs of hot chocolate. Jill swapped my empty mug for one of the fresh mugs as Lance helped remove her tank. Rachel took the other cup after removing her own gear. "We saw nothing," she said.

Lance gestured for me to open my dive bag. I pulled out a few small bones, then the ring which had sunk to the bottom of the bag. Rachel looked at the bones, then at me. "You found those?"

"After Lance found an arm bone."

She turned to Parker. "Have you got this spot logged into the GPS?"

"Yep, I created a waypoint. We can come back to this exact spot whenever we want."

Rachel picked up a cubic bone and turned it in her fingers. "This looks like a Carpal bone, from the wrist." She spread the other bones out on top of the bag. "I see more carpals, a couple of metacarpals, which run from the wrist to the fingers. The rest are phalanges and finger bones. It'll take an ME to figure out which bones go with which finger. One is obviously from a ring finger."

Jill picked up the ring and turned it. "This isn't a wedding band. It's got some sort of weird triangle emblem that's mostly worn away." She looked at it from a different angle. "There might be a skull at the bottom of the triangle. It might be a biker theme."

"Maybe it's unique enough that someone could identify it," I suggested.

"It would be asking too much for it to be engraved with the owner's name, address, and phone number," Rachel joked.

Jill handed the ring to her. "I don't see any engraving inside."

"You're right, this triangle thing is odd, as is the tiny skull." Rachel said, turning the ring so the spot was in the sunlight. "There's one tiny mark inside of it. I think it says 14k. This isn't some cheap ring out of a gum machine."

She handed it back to me. "What do you think?"

I held the ring at arm's length, where it was in focus. "I can't make it out."

Lance laughed. "Do you want to borrow my reading glasses, grandpa?"

A smile spread across Jill's face. "That's it, isn't it? You need reading glasses."

"I can see my computer just fine."

"But you needed me to tell you how many Sudafed to take when you had a cold."

Interrupting us, Rachel said, "You'd better stow that ring and the bones, so they don't get bounced out of the boat on our way back to town."

Lance topped off our hot chocolate, then confirmed that the gear was properly strapped in place. He retrieved the dive flag, started the engine and turned the boat toward town. We motored slowly, at a speed that didn't spill our hot chocolate, as we cut through the waves.

# Chapter 5

We changed out of the wetsuits at the fire station while Parker brewed a pot of coffee. I let the shower's hot water pound on my back. As my arms and legs warmed, it must've released a rush of cold blood because I broke into shivers and my teeth chattered like they hadn't since I was a teen.

Everett, the three firemen, and Jill, who was wrapped in a wool blanket, were sitting at a table in the firehouse kitchen. Vic English was leaning against the counter. He smiled at me and raised his cup. "It sounds like you guys were successful."

I nodded and poured myself a cup of coffee. "What brings you to the fire hall, Vic?"

"I was having coffee with the boys and saw the Park Service pickup parked over here. I thought I'd check to see if you guys were joining the fire department or taking a tour."

Rachel rolled her eyes. "Vic lives his life vicariously through our exploits. He's sitting here with a fresh pot of coffee brewed every time we return from a call out."

"Just looking out for my comrades in the fire department."

Rachel looked at me. "He has no life."

That comment appeared to strike home, as Vic changed the topic. "What did you find out from old Mischke?"

"We haven't had a chance to talk to him yet. That's our next project."

Vic nodded, then dumped the dregs of his coffee into the sink and rinsed his cup. "Are you guys planning to dive again tomorrow?"

Rachel glared at him and nodded toward Lance and Parker. "*Us guys* have regular jobs. Besides, a storm is blowing in. I'm not taking the boat out in four-foot waves unless it's for a rescue call."

"Wimps. That's barely a walleye chop."

Lance glanced at Vic. "There are plenty of city folk who believe that shit. They get up here for three or four days and decide they *have to* fish regardless of the weather. I swear some of those idiots would try to fish during a hurricane."

Vic leaned close to me as he passed. "You guys need to jack up these firemen. Once word gets around that you've found more of the skeleton, there will be idiots out there trying to find the skull before you do. And I don't think they'll turn it in. It'll end up...in some pagan ritual or something."

Rachel watched the exchange between Vic and me. When he left, she walked to the sink to wash her cup. "Watch out for Vic. He thinks he's still a cop."

Parker nodded. "He's a real pain in the ass. The police chief chews him out every time there's a new cop in town. Vic has nothing to do, so he spends a lot of time following the rookies around and offering *suggestions*. The chief is the field training officer, and Vic suggests outdated procedures that don't follow department policies. That doesn't go over well with the FTO."

"Vic is undeterred?" I asked.

"Vic is Vic. He's an expert on any topic you care to discuss and will tell you exactly what's needed to correct whatever's wrong."

Rachel knelt next to Jill and rubbed her shoulder. "Are you warm yet? I think you have a touch of hypothermia."

Jill shrugged off the blanket and handed it to her. "Thanks. I'm doing better."

"Don't worry, Rachel. She'll warm up her feet on me when we're in bed tonight."

Parker laughed. "Gee, that sounds romantic."

"There's nothing romantic about it," Jill explained. "Doug has excess body heat. He shares it with me."

"I could think of a couple of other approaches for body heat transfer," Lance offered.

Rachel cut him off. "Enough schoolyard stupidity. You two wouldn't know romance if it came up and kissed you on the lips."

Lance was about to throw out a witty reply when Rachel raised one finger. "One more word and you'll be washing the fire trucks for the next month."

Parker smiled. "Thank you, Chief."

Jill turned to Rachel. "You're the fire chief?"

"I'm the chief because I'm often the only adult in the room."

"And she can write a grant proposal. If not for her, we'd still be driving a 1968 truck that only started if you gave it a shot of ether," Parker counted off her other contributions on his fingers, from the air tank filling system to the reflective fire number signs, coats, uniforms, and a 911 text relay system for calls.

Rachel, wearing a smug smile, listened with her arms crossed.

"You're the glue that holds this department together," Jill suggested.

"There were a couple of old-school guys who didn't like the way I ran things and left. They were replaced by some new folks who have their shit together and know how to be team players."

Lance straightened up. "Are you saying Parker and I are team players?"

Rachel smiled. "You two show up every time I ask for a favor. Like looking for bones on the bottom of the lake."

"Damn, Parker. We're part of the team."

Everett had been listening quietly. He checked his watch, then picked up Jill's cup and washed it. "Unless there's something pressing, I need to have Doug and Jill back to Davidson's by five."

Rachel frowned. "Is there a Park Service curfew?"

Jill glanced at Everett, who read her thoughts about outing his date plans, and blushed. She stated, "The kitchen sometimes runs out of the daily special, and we don't want to miss the walleye tonight."

Sensing the fiction in Jill's comment, Rachel said, "That'd be something, a northern Minnesota resort's kitchen running out of the most popular item on the menu."

* * *

On our way out of town, Everett looked at Jill in the mirror. "Thanks for not outing my dating plans to the firemen."

"No problem," Jill replied. "Not that they don't already know who's dating and where they go. It's a small town."

"What was that comment Vic made about talking to Mischke?" Everett asked.

Jill explained, "The machinist/welder lost his boat anchor. He'd welded his initials on the anchor, and we're going to talk to him about the details, then compare what he says to the anchor tied to the foot."

"I've got the ME's pictures of the anchor, rope, and foot on my laptop. I'll bring it along when I pick you up tomorrow."

I thought about that for a moment, then said, "Vic wasn't there when we talked about the anchor."

"Small town."

I shook my head. "There were only four of us in the room during that discussion. I can't imagine Davidson talking about it."

Everett interrupted our discussion by pointing to a narrow dirt road. He slowed so we could see a signpost covered with arrows painted with family names. "Those are all the people with homes or cabins down there. Mischke's machine shop is at the end of the road."

Jill was trying to do something on her phone in the back seat. "The cell service is spotty out here."

"It depends on your cell phone carrier. Some have better range than others. All the towers are in I-Falls, and there are gaps in between. If you want to contact someone, you might be best off texting."

"I was trying to Google something."

"Your best bet for internet access is using the resort Wi-Fi when we get back there."

Everett stopped at our cabin. "Eight o'clock again tomorrow?" he asked.

"That sounds good," I replied. "Remember your laptop so we can look at the ME's pictures."

"Where are you meeting Laney?" Jill asked.

Everett nodded toward the resort entrance. "She shares a cabin on Wood Tick Alley with three other girls."

"They named a road Wood Tick Alley?"

"It's just a driveway to the staff cabins. The girls call it Wood Tick Alley. They're collecting all of the wood ticks they pick off after walking the trail through the woods. They've got a jar with alcohol on the kitchen counter."

"Have they collected many?" I asked.

"They've got about a half inch so far."

Jill froze. "They've got a jar with a half-inch thick layer of dead wood ticks on their kitchen counter?"

"Yeah."

"How many years has it taken to collect that many ticks?"

"That's just since the resort opened in mid-May."

We wished Everett goodnight and walked to our cabin. "I can feel wood ticks crawling on me," Jill said as she squirmed.

"Tell you what, strip naked and I'll search for ticks."

"I'll let you check my back. The rest I'll handle."

"Killjoy."

Jill went into the bathroom immediately and locked the door. I lifted my pants legs and checked my ankles. Having spent no time walking through the grass, I was reasonably certain we wouldn't have any ticks. I was checking out the cable television channels when Jill emerged.

She sat on my lap and snuggled. "I'm still cold."

I pulled her close and rubbed her back. "Let's eat supper at the lodge. We can come back here, climb under the quilt, and watch television."

She pulled me tight. "I'm too cold to think about romance." With those words, she jumped up and grabbed a sweatshirt. "Come on. Supper awaits."

Two fishermen from the next-door cabin walked with us to the lodge. They'd had a slow day of fishing and asked our opinion about hiring a guide to find the fish. I plead ignorance and suggested they speak with Max Davidson.

The dining room/bar seemed busy for a weeknight, and we waited for the servers to clean one of the high-top tables for us. Jill slid onto the stool and frowned. "I prefer padded chairs to sitting on these wooden stools."

"Maybe you need to add some padding to your skinny butt," I whispered.

"Very funny, Fletcher."

Megan, our server from the other evening, turned away from the table next to us and smiled. "Would you like to order something to drink, or would you prefer I come back after you finish the skinny butt discussion?"

Jill hung her head, then started laughing. "How many personal discussions do you stumble into a night?"

"It kind of depends. I don't mind you guys kidding around. I hate the arguments."

We ordered Diet Cokes and looked at the menu. Megan was back in less than a minute. "Tonight's special is an eight-ounce sirloin steak with salad and baked potato." After pausing, she leaned close and whispered, "Skip the steak and order from the menu."

Jill handed me her menu and ordered a pulled pork sandwich with slaw and fries.

"I think I'll go with the California burger again, with fries, not poutine." Megan noted our order and disappeared into the kitchen.

The crowd wasn't rowdy, but the acoustics were terrible, causing everyone to speak loud enough to be heard over the neighboring tables. I looked around the room to see if there was anyone who made me uneasy. The crowd was mostly fishermen, with a table of women who appeared to be local folks who were out for the evening rather than resort people.

"Check out the guy at the end of the bar," Jill whispered. She nodded to the corner behind me.

I pretended to drop my paper napkin and had to reach under the table to retrieve it. As I stood, I looked at the older guy with his hands wrapped around a beer mug. His face was sunburned and covered with white scars, probably from skin cancer removal. His sunburn ended abruptly on his forehead, where his hat had covered his head. His shirt looked worn, and he seemed out of place among the fishermen wearing name-brand clothing.

"I suppose he's a local fisherman. Maybe he guides for the resort."

Jill glanced over my shoulder at the man, then leaned close. "He's talking to himself. It seems like he's becoming more agitated."

"We can't solve all of the world's problems. Keep an eye on him, but let's let him be."

When Megan delivered out dinners, I asked about the lone man. She glanced at the bar, then leaned close. "That's Booger."

"You call him Booger?" Jill asked.

"God, no! Not to his face. I've heard his name is Russian or Hungarian, Kovacs or Serlick, or something."

"Is he a regular?"

"He wanders in several nights a week. Sometimes he orders a burger. Other nights, like tonight, he just nurses a beer."

"He's talking to himself."

Megan nodded. "He's a conspiracy theorist. Most women kind of avoid talking to him because he's kind of off the wall. Some of the fishermen think he's entertaining."

"Why do you call him Booger?" Jill asked.

"I'd rather not get into his nasal secretions. Do you guys need anything else?"

Megan rushed to a table where someone had spilled a beer. Jill ate but kept glancing at Booger. "That could be you twenty years from now."

"What are you talking about?"

"A sad old guy who's paranoid about everything. Sitting in a bar with a beer in front of you while you talk to yourself because everyone thinks you're crazy."

"Thanks for that vote of confidence."

Jill smiled. "No problem."

Halfway through her sandwich, Jill glanced at Booger and froze. "Uh oh."

"What?"

"Booger saw me watching him. He seems more agitated."

"Jeez, stop making eye contact. Ignore him."

"Too late. He's walking this way with his beer."

Booger stood at the end of our table and glanced at me before fixing his eyes on Jill. "I see your badge."

"We're Park Service investigators," she replied.

"Feds?"

Feeling the need to break Booger's eye contact with Jill, I replied, "We're federal law enforcement officers. We're here to investigate the foot that was found attached to an anchor in the national park."

Booger turned to me and stared as if he was about to say something. When the staring had gone on too long, I asked, "Do you know anything about that foot and anchor?"

"Isn't it obvious?"

"Not to us," I replied. "Please fill us in."

Booger looked around the dining room, apparently checking to see if anyone was watching or listening to us. "The government killed him."

"Which government?"

The question seemed to surprise Booger. "Our government. You know, the deep state. They spy on us, and if we get too close to understanding what's happening, they kill us." Booger suddenly straightened up. "Wait. You're feds. Are you spying on me? I've seen the drones watching. I thought it would only be a matter of time until they sent someone to deal with me."

"The drones have been watching you?"

Booger leaned close. "They look like seagulls."

"The drones look like seagulls? How do you tell the drones from the real seagulls?"

"The drones don't eat fish."

"Do you live nearby?" I asked.

That question seemed to stump Booger. "If you're federal agents, you already know where I live. You've been spying on me for years."

"We work for the US National Park Service. We don't do surveillance on anyone."

"I sincerely doubt that. How do you know who starts forest fires? How do you know when someone shoots a wolf?"

"I think you have us confused with the Forest Service and the Fish and Wildlife Service. We deal with crimes committed inside national parks."

"Do you watch television?"

"Not a lot. Why? Is there something special we should be watching?"

"Your television has a camera that watches you even when it's turned off. You need to put a piece of tin foil over the camera lens."

"Where is the camera?" I whispered.

"It's that little red light in the corner. They want you to think it's an on/off indicator, but it's a camera lens. The other thing you can do is to unplug it when you turn it off. That disables the camera too."

"Do you live nearby?" I asked.

"Just past the end of the parking lot and down the path about fifty yards. I keep a kerosene lantern burning at night, in case you want to come over."

My mind nearly exploded when I thought about all of the crackpot stuff Booger might have around his house. "I think we'll have to pass on your offer this trip."

"It's your loss. I have some beavertail smoking out back. There's hardly anything that tastes better than that."

"I gave up beavertail for Lent," I replied.

Jill frowned and mouthed *Lent?*

Booger nodded his understanding. "I appreciate a man who takes God into his heart. Bless you."

"We think the guy who was found tied to the anchor might've been there since 1989. What do you think about that?"

Booger considered the question for a moment. "In 1987, Reagan took responsibility for the Iran-Contra deal."

I shrugged. "I suppose that could be true. I'm more concerned about this body that was dumped in Black Bay in '89. The police think it might've been a guy who was killed at the motel in town."

Booger paused, then got a strange look on his face. He turned toward Jill, hesitated, then sneezed, spraying her leg. Without acknowledging Jill's snotty leg, he pulled a crusty bandana from his pocket and blew his nose, which could pass as a moose call. After jamming the bandana back in his pocket, Booger stared at me as Megan rushed over with a bar rag to wipe Jill's pant leg.

"There were guys cooking meth in Miller's cabin before it burned down. I think they were even more paranoid than I was. I went over to complain about the ammonia smell, and they ran me off with a shotgun. I snuck back there a couple of nights and listened to them talking around their campfire. Someone named Santos got greedy and they cut him out."

"Cut him out as in threw him out of the gang?"

"Cut him out, as in they split his share of whatever they were making."

"You snuck up on a bunch of drug dealers?" I asked, thinking that was unlikely.

Booger glanced at Jill, then leaned close to me. "Were you in the Army?"

"Yeah, I was deployed in Iraq."

"I was a tunnel rat in Vietnam. I could sneak up on a guy eating his lunch in the tunnel, slit his throat, and slip away without the guy sitting next to him knowing I'd been there."

"You were one badass sonofabitch," I said, shaking his hand. "Thanks for your service."

"A fat lot of good it did me. The doctors are carving cancer out of me every year, and the Army refuses to admit it's because of the Agent Orange they used to coat the countryside."

"What's your name?"

Booger froze. "Are you going to report me?"

"Report you for what?"

"Disabling your drones. Unplugging my TV so they can't spy on me. Eating beaver taken out of season."

"How do you disable drones?"

"Twelve gauge with number six shot." Booger sighed and looked down. "You're here to arrest me for that, aren't you?"

"I'm not the drone police, and I'm not here to arrest you. Tell me your name."

Booger scanned the faces around us. "You already know my name, or you wouldn't be here."

I decided to try a different approach. "I want to use you as a confidential informant. What should I call you?"

He thought for a second while weighing what I'd said. "Call me Booger, like the waitresses and bartender do."

I pulled out a twenty-dollar bill and waved it at the bartender. "I'm buying Booger's beer tonight."

The bartender frowned and replied, "He's already covered."

"Then, this is for tomorrow's beer."

"Why do you want me to be your informant?"

"I need to know more about the foot tied to the anchor. You're my local information source. Do you remember back to 1989 when the guy was killed in the motel?"

Booger looked at the windows where the twilight had turned the clouds orange. "Like I said, *if* that really happened, it was the meth head's doing."

"Did they dump his body into the lake with the anchor tied to his foot?"

"If that happened at night, no one would've seen them dump him."

A group of men seated at a table near the door broke out in laughter. One made a big deal out of checking his watch, then announcing it was time to get their gear into the boat. "The walleyes will be biting as soon as it's dark."

"Maybe a fisherman saw them make the dump." Seeing no recognition of that event, I added, "Or saw them transporting the body to Black Bay."

Frowning, Booger considered the situation as a drip of snot formed on the tip of his nose. Jill slid away from him to avoid being sprayed by another sneeze. After wiping the drip on his sleeve, he asked, "Why would drug addicts drag a body all the way from town to Black Bay? That's an hour or more round-trip with a fishing boat. I'd think they'd stay within sight of town so they wouldn't get lost or run their boat onto some underwater rock pile."

Having been focused on Vic's story about the bloody discovery in town had diverted me from the obvious. No indigent, drug dealer, or petty criminal would transport a body all the way from I-Falls to Black Bay. We'd passed dozens of little inlets on our trip to the search area. Any of them would've been a simple location for a dump-and-run.

A different question sprang to mind. "How far is Mischke's place from town or Black Bay?"

"What's Mischke got to do with this?"

"We think his boat might've been used to transport the body."

Booger sniffled, then took a sip of beer. "Mischke's place is at the end of the road. Nobody is going to drive to his place, walk past his house, then steal his boat from the dock. There are probably a hundred boats that would've been easier to steal from town."

"Who would use Mischke's boat to dispose of a body?"

The question obviously stumped Booger, who stared at his beer. His head jerked up as his eyes lit up. "It's obvious! It had to be the feds. They saw something going on at Mischke's and wanted to frame him for a murder. Think about it. Mischke. Doesn't that name sound Russian?"

Jill's grin expressed her opinion of that scenario.

"I have the feeling that Mischke has had his place on Rainy Lake for a long time. I doubt he's a Russian undercover operative."

"Russia put deep spies in place during the Cold War. Owning a machine shop on Rainy Lake would be a great cover. Hell, old Mischke has probably been smuggling Russian agents across the border from Canada for decades." Booger paused to wipe another drip on his sleeve. "Think about it, Mr. Fed. You may have found a Russian sleeper spy ring!"

Booger's last comment brought looks from a dozen nearby people. Most stared for a second, smiled or laughed, and went back to their discussions.

"Let's suppose that's not what happened. Why would someone else choose to dump a body tied to an anchor in Black Bay?"

Being totally convinced by his last theory, Booger just shook his head.

Jill leaned on the table and said, "Sometimes the simplest explanation is the correct answer."

"I'm not aware of a simple answer."

"Maybe Mischke dumped the body?"

"When did all this happen?" Booger asked.

"The motel murder was in 1989. We think Mischke's boat was stolen at the same time." At that point, I saw the jump I'd made in assumptions. "We're not sure when Mischke's boat was stolen. It was a long time ago, and that could be an incident separated by days, months, or years."

I looked at Jill, who raised her eyebrows and cocked her head. "They may be totally unrelated crimes. Hell, maybe neither of them is related to the body in Black Bay."

Booger stared at me, waiting for a response. When I didn't say anything, he sniffled, then drank the last of his beer. "This resort is the only public launch on Black Bay. There are a couple dozen houses and cabins on the bay, too. You could launch a canoe almost anywhere along the shore."

"Thanks for making me take a step back. You're a valuable confidential informant."

Booger reached out his deeply tanned and beer-stained hand he'd used to wipe his nose. "You're okay for a fed."

Without hesitation, I shook his hand. "I've heard that before." As soon as he released his grip, I felt the need to rush to the restroom to wash my hands before I touched anything.

He turned to Jill, who quickly stuffed both of her hands into her pockets. "You're too pretty to be a fed." With that, he left.

"Why do I only get compliments from grungy old men? That happened in the Black Hills, too."

"I think you're pretty, too."

Jill got a lopsided grin that formed one dimple and replied, "We've already determined you need glasses."

Megan returned with our check. As she cleared the dishes, she whispered, "You guys handled Booger really well. He sometimes gets agitated when people argue with him."

Jill leaned close to Megan and whispered, "He knows that you guys call him Booger."

She blushed. "OMG. I feel terrible."

"It's now his code name."

* * *

Because we were approaching the summer solstice, the longest day of the year, twilight lingered. As we walked from the lodge to our cabin, the sky went from purple to black. Just as we stepped out of the parking lot onto the path, a distant howl pierced the quiet night. As she had when the coyotes howled in Arizona, Jill grabbed my arm.

"That's not a coyote," I observed. "It's a deeper, more resonant wolf howl." A moment later, a responding howl came from a different direction.

She held out her arm, showing me her goosebumps backlit by the lodge lights. "That's not helpful, dear. I don't like coyotes or wolves and telling me there are timber wolves close enough to hear is not reassuring." She tugged at my arm, speeding up our pace.

"Take it easy, you're carrying a firearm," I reassured her.

"Great! I can see like five or ten feet. How long would it take a charging wolf to cover that distance? Hmm? Less time than it would take for me to draw my Glock."

"When I was in Boy Scouts, we were told there had never been a documented case of a wolf attacking a human."

"That's because the victims all died! There was no one to report the attack!"

Back in our cabin, Jill showered while I flipped through the cable television options. Billows of steam emerged when she, wrapped in a bath towel, opened the bathroom door. "My goosebumps are gone and I'm finally warm." She pulled pajamas from the suitcase and slipped back into the bathroom to change.

"Too bad you can't schedule a hot flash for the times you're chilled."

"That's not how they work. I'm usually already hot when they show up. It's been a while since I've had one." She dashed out of the bathroom, flipped back the covers, and quickly pulled them over herself. "These sheets are frigid. Get in here and warm me up."

I took off my shirt and pants, then slid under the covers. Jill threw her arm over my chest and pulled me close as she put her cold feet on my calves.

"How can you be warm?" she asked. "We were both chilled to the bone."

"I was only moderately chilled. I think you were past that point. It takes a couple of days to recover from hypothermia."

"Turn onto your side so we can spoon." She pressed herself against me and hugged.

"What do you think about Booger's comments?"

"He has a point. Drug addicts and petty criminals wouldn't steal a boat and travel miles in the dark to dump a body. Something else is going on."

"It'll be interesting to see if the ME can get enough DNA from any of the bones to compare to the federal database."

"The ring you found was weird. Maybe it's distinctive enough to point to the owner."

I rolled over so we were facing each other. "When we first met, we didn't lie in bed talking about dead people. You're turning into a cop."

"As I listened to Booger, I pictured him at home wearing an aluminum foil hat."

"Yeah, he's out there. On the other hand, he made a great point about the killer not transporting a body from I-Falls to Black Bay by boat."

Jill was silent for so long I thought she might've fallen asleep. Her eyes popped open, and she lifted her head. "Booger said, *if* Vic's story about the bloody motel scene is true."

"Vic's an ex-cop. I have no reason to doubt his veracity. And let's face it, Booger might not be the most reliable source of information."

"Just the same, he is not entirely convinced there was a bloody motel killing. I wonder what other people think about that?"

# Chapter 6

We finished breakfast and were drinking coffee when Everett walked in. He waved to us, then nodded to Laney. Instead of rushing over with a cup of coffee for him, she looked away, then walked into the kitchen.

Jill read more into that move than I did. "Something changed last night."

Everett looked confused. "Huh? With the case?"

"Between you and Laney."

Everett glanced at the kitchen door. "Oh, that," he said as he blushed.

Seeing no point in torturing Everett, I said, "We talked to an old timer who was sitting at the bar last night. He pointed out that it was unlikely a bunch of druggies would kill someone in I-Falls, put their body into a boat, and transport them all the way to the park when they could just as easily dump the body a dozen places closer to town. He also questioned how they would steal Mischke's boat from a house that's literally at the end of the road."

The kitchen door opened, and Laney backed through while carrying a tray. Ignoring her, I added, "He suggested it was more likely that the body wasn't dumped from Mischke's boat, or that Mischke was involved."

Laney leaned the tray on the table next to us and placed a platter with pancakes, eggs, and sausage in front of Everett. Her smile said she only had eyes for him. "You probably need to keep your strength up," she said before pouring coffee for him and topping off our cups.

Jill hid her grin by lifting the coffee cup to her lips. Everett smiled at Laney, then glanced at me, looking like he'd just committed a crime.

I jumped in, trying to break up whatever was happening between them. "Laney, tell us about Booger."

My question snapped her out of whatever lovesick trance she'd been in. "Booger?"

"The old guy who sits alone at the end of the bar talking about conspiracy theories."

"Oh, him."

"What do you know about him?"

"I try not to know anything about him. I mean, he's creepy, and his nose is always running. He's disgusting."

"Does he live nearby?"

"I guess so. Someone said he walks here, so he can't live very far away."

"Does he always talk about government drones and conspiracies?"

"I try not to listen. He babbles on like a right-wing radio station."

I heard the cook yell, "Order up!" from the kitchen. Laney ran her fingers through the hair on the nape of Everett's neck as she walked past. The move caused Everett to concentrate on his pancakes and avoid eye contact with us.

"You're allowed to have a girlfriend," Jill said.

Everett wiped syrup from his lip and stared at Jill for a second. "It's not going to interfere with my work with you. I promise."

"That's probably not a problem," I said. "The beauty of working on cold cases is that the hours are regular and there's not a lot of nighttime surveillance or shootouts."

Everett straightened up and adjusted his bulletproof vest. "Shootouts? We work for the Park Service, not the DEA or FBI hostage rescue team."

"We still qualify with our weapons and are sworn to uphold the law and Constitution. That sometimes means drawing your weapon and being prepared to use it."

"Theoretically."

"Actually," Jill replied.

Everett reached down for a backpack he'd set on the floor. "I found a state trooper who was going to Duluth last night. He delivered the bones to the medical examiner.

There's obviously no analysis of them yet, but I downloaded pictures of the foot and anchor. I also took pictures of the ring you found."

He booted up his computer and showed us four pictures of the anchor and assorted foot and ankle bones. I moved through the anchor pictures and stopped at one showing the initials RM. I turned the computer so Jill could look. "It appears that Mischke's anchor has been found."

"We were going to talk to him anyway," Jill replied. "Now we can show him that his missing anchor has been found."

I looked at the pictures of the ring. The surface was scratched and worn so much of the detail was lost. As Jill had described it, there was a triangle with a rounded top. At the bottom of the triangle was a skull. I studied it, racking my brain trying to recall where I'd seen a similar symbol.

"What are you thinking? Is this some sort of gang symbol?" Jill asked.

"It's familiar. Maybe military?"

"Military, with a death's head?" Jill asked. "Gestapo?"

"No, American military." I studied the picture, trying to pick up any of the details that had apparently been worn away over time. "Someone had worn this for a long time. And this had meaning for the wearer. Indigent people aren't sentimental. The hardcore homeless folks would pawn their mother's engagement ring for a bottle of booze."

"Email those photos to me, please," Jill took out her phone and hooked up to the resort Wi-Fi as Everett worked his way through the stack of cakes and eggs. Laney checked on us and topped off our coffee.

"I'm doing a search for military emblems with skulls." She turned her phone so Everett and I could see the screen. "There are dozens of military rings with skulls on them. Here are Army, Marine Corps, and Navy rings with skulls."

"None from the Air Force or Coast Guard?" I joked.

"Not funny, Fletcher," Jill replied as she took her phone back. She changed the search and waited for the results to load. "I changed the parameters to USMC. None of these has anything resembling a triangle."

"Try the Army."

Jill shook her head. "I've got helmets, crossed swords, crossed rifles, and a skull with a dagger in its teeth. That's special forces."

"Airborne!" I said. "The triangle is an open parachute!"

Jill typed in airborne and a second later, she smiled. "Bingo!" She turned the phone so we could see an airborne ring with an open parachute and a skull where the parachute cords came together.

"Our guy had been airborne qualified by the Army," she said, saving the search.

"Or, his father or grandfather were," Everett suggested.

"Let's assume the ring belonged to the guy who was wearing it. That means if the ME can get DNA from the bones, he'll be able to compare it to the Armed Forces DNA database and identify our victim."

Everett pushed his plate away. "What does that buy us?"

I patted his shoulder. "Nearly all murderers are known to their victims. Knowing who the victim is narrows the field of potential killers a lot."

Something we'd said struck a chord with Jill, who was now staring out of the windows. "Booger was in Vietnam. You don't think..."

I shook my head. "Booger told me he was a tunnel rat in Vietnam. I don't think the Army used airborne troops to root out the tunnels." I paused. "Who knows. I saw enough in Iraq to know the Army does what the Army wants to do, and a lot of it only makes sense to someone far above my pay grade."

Laney came back and asked, "Can I get you anything else?"

"Charge it to our cabin and add a nice tip."

Laney smiled at Everett, who was packing up his computer. "How nice a tip are we talking about?"

"Thirty percent," Jill replied as she stood.

Laney had just turned away when I stopped her. "Have you ever noticed Booger wearing a ring?"

She snorted. "I can't imagine him married. Can you?"

"I was thinking about a military ring, maybe something he'd wear on his right hand."

"I've never paid any attention to Booger's hands." Her scowl turned into a smile as she turned to Everett. "Pizza again tonight, or did you have something else in mind?"

"I need to see if Doug and Jill need me to do something with them."

Jill patted his shoulder. "We'll keep ourselves occupied. You're free to do whatever you want after you drop us off."

Everett shrugged. "Pizza is okay. Or we could go out for burgers."

"I can get burgers here anytime," Laney said with a smile. "I'd rather have pizza...and dessert."

I urged Everett toward the door. "And dessert?"

Red crept up Everett's neck, and he rushed to the pickup without saying anything.

"How far away is Mischke's machine shop?" I asked as we pulled away from the lodge.

"I've never actually driven down that road. There are signs for like twelve houses or cabins, and I know the machine shop is at the end of the road. I suppose we're five miles from the turn and the shop is maybe half a mile down the road."

"How far is it from his shop to where the bones were found?"

"Across the water?"

"Yeah. If you took a boat between those spots, how long would it take?"

Everett tried to picture the lake. "If he's got a fifty-horse motor, he could probably cross the bay in less than ten minutes."

"In twenty minutes, he could cross the bay, dump the body, and be back home."

"About that."

"Add two minutes for tying the rope around the ankle," Jill added.

Her comment fired an odd thought. "Let me see the anchor pictures again."

Jill pulled the photos up, and I flipped to the picture that showed the knotted rope. "Whoever tied this guy to the anchor knew how to tie a knot."

"It looks like a granny knot to me."

"No, the knot was tied from a loop of anchor rope. Look at how the double strands are parallel, going into the loop, and around, leaving a nice loop to slip a foot into. The guy who did this was a sailor or rock climber."

Jill leaned over the seat and studied the image. "Fletcher, how do you know that?"

"When I was in scouts, we spent hours learning to tie knots. This is not a simple knot to tie, and the guy who did it takes pride in his knots."

Everett shrugged. "I suppose a lot of the folks around the lake know how to tie knots like that."

"I disagree. I doubt there are a dozen people on all of Rainy Lake who know how to tie this knot."

"What's it called?" Jill asked.

I closed the file. "I can't remember. But that may be a way of narrowing the list of suspects. The guy who tied this will know what it's called."

Jill leaned back. "So, we're going to stop at every boat launch, resort, and cabin until we find a guy who can tell us what this knot is called?"

"How do we know a guy tied this knot?" Everett asked.

I glanced at Jill. "What's the answer?"

"Most women don't have the stomach to tie an anchor to someone's leg and toss them overboard. It's a guy thing." She paused, then added, "In the old days, they called poison the women's weapon. A woman can poison someone and walk away. Men tend to be violent and prefer to bludgeon, stab, or strangle their victims."

Everett glanced at Jill in the mirror. "Really? I didn't learn that in criminology."

Chuckling, I said, "That's because they didn't assign any books by Sir Arthur Conan Doyle." Seeing Everett's lost look, I explained, "Jill is a big fan of Sherlock Holmes."

"Is he that guy played by Benedict Cumberbatch? He and Martin Freeman run around England solving old mysteries."

"Yes," Jill replied. "That's Sherlock Holmes."

"Isn't he like, made up? I mean, those aren't real stories."

I chuckled. "The beauty of modeling your investigations after fictional characters is that every mystery is solved before the show is over. Those detectives have a one-hundred percent closure rate. And often in sixty to ninety minutes."

"Are you making fun of Jill?"

"Not at all. I think it's funny that she uses a fictional nineteenth-century detective as her fallback source of police procedure and knowledge."

I glanced at Jill, who was sticking her tongue out at me. "How often have I been wrong in citing Sherlock? Don't you agree that women prefer poison to bludgeoning or stabbing their victims? Hmm?"

"I'll use my own nineteenth-century example. 'Lizzie Borden took an axe, gave her mother forty whacks. When she saw what she had done, she gave her father forty-one.'"

"Ha! That's pure fiction. They never proved that Lizzie killed them!"

Everett glanced at me, then at Jill. "Do you two always argue like this?"

"Are we making you nervous?" Jill asked.

"Not nervous. It's more like...I don't know. It's weird." He paused, then asked, "Do you two always work together?"

"We're assigned as an investigative team," I replied.

"Why?"

From the back seat, Jill replied, "Because they sometimes need someone who can be diplomatic, like me, to balance the bull in the China shop Doug."

Everett glanced at me. "Is that true?"

"I can be as delicate as I need to be, or I can charge ahead when the situation demands it."

Everett turned onto the narrow, muddy road leading to the machine shop. Trees brushed against the pickup's mirrors, and the pickup rocked as we splashed through potholes in the gravel.

"They need to grade this road," Jill commented.

"I think they leave it like this to discourage casual visitors," I observed. "No one comes down here without a reason."

We passed driveways marked only by fire number signs. Each disappeared into the underbrush without providing a view of the structure. "This is what the Twin Cities folks refer to as 'the boonies.'"

About a mile into the drive, the forest thinned, and we entered a clearing. The driveway was marked by a rusty six-foot diameter saw blade with Mischke Machine painted in white letters. A house with weathered cedar siding was flanked by a pole barn. The barn doors were open, and the area around the barn was cluttered with a variety of machines, apparently in different states of repair. The grass had grown up around some of them, making me think that they might be past the point of repair.

Everett parked alongside the barn, and we were greeted by a yellow lab with a wagging tail. "Hey, pal," I said, holding out my hand. "You look happy to see me. Are you?"

Jill knelt down, and the dog rushed to her with its tongue lolling. "Hey, buddy. How are you?" she asked as she scratched the dog's ears vigorously.

"Do all animals like Jill?" Everett asked.

"Dogs, people, and horses seem to."

Jill looked up as a man emerged from the barn. His face was covered in soot, as were his coveralls and gloves. He glared at us. "You ain't the guy who's going to fix my furnace." He studied Everett's uniform for a moment, then glanced at my holster and badge as I swatted a mosquito that was biting my neck.

"We found your anchor," I said, opening Everett's folder. I held out the picture. "This is yours, right? With the RM welded on the anchor?"

"Where in hell did you find this? It's been missing for...phew, forty years."

Out of the corner of my eye, I saw Jill waving her hand to chase away the mosquitoes hovering around her head. "It was on the other side of the bay."

Mischke cocked his head as he pulled off the sooty gloves he used to swat a mosquito. "What's the Park Service care about my lost anchor?"

I handed him another picture, showing the anchor rope around the ankle. "It appears the anchor was used to weigh a body down."

Mischke was either a great actor, or he was genuinely surprised by the news. "My anchor?"

I nodded. "The anchor in the picture."

"Who?"

"We don't know. Do you have any candidates?"

The machinist pulled off his dirty cap, exposing his bald head, which immediately attracted mosquitoes. "I...got nothing." He looked at me. "Am I a suspect?"

"I'm not ruling anyone in or out. At this point, I'm just asking questions."

Mischke nodded toward the house. "You folks got time for a cup of coffee? We gotta get away from these skeeters. Besides, my wife is probably wondering what's going on."

The dog beat us to the house and was first to scoot through when Mischke opened the door. Jill stepped in first, and we all paused in the mud room to take off our dirty shoes and to swat a few more mosquitoes.

I was focused on untying my shoe when the dog walked over and licked my ear.

Surprised, I jerked my head away and laughed. "Doggy kisses."

Mischke smiled. "Queenie, come over here. I'm not sure our guests are up for your affection."

Queenie didn't move. When I tried to urge her to go away, she started wagging her tail, which thumped against Jill's leg.

A woman called the dog from an adjacent room, and Queenie bounded up the three steps and disappeared into the kitchen. Peggy Mischke, with a round, florid face and a big smile, introduced herself and gestured to the kitchen table. She apologized as she set a package of Oreos on the table, explaining she hadn't had time to bake. Randy explained the discovery of his long-missing anchor as she poured coffee for us.

"Somebody tied Randy's anchor to some poor soul's leg and dumped him into the lake? That's terrible."

"Do you remember exactly when your boat and anchor disappeared?"

Randy leaned back. "Phew! It was in the '80s." He ran his hand over his bald head as he thought. "It was after the fishing opener. I remember because I used to guide a few people in the early season, and I'd finished up with them before the boat disappeared." He looked at Peggy. "Do you recall, Peg?"

Peggy made a dismissive gesture. "I don't get involved in fishing or the machine shop."

"It might've been about the same time they were investigating a possible murder at the motel in town," I suggested.

Peggy sat down, and Queenie immediately put her chin on the woman's thigh. Petting as she thought, Peggy frowned. "I just don't recall. That was a long time ago, and I was busy raising kids."

I looked at Randy, hoping he'd connect the events. Instead, he shook his head. "I suppose it might've been about then. I don't know."

"Do you remember any problems with people cooking meth in that time frame?"

Randy snorted. "They blew up or burned down some cabin south of us. Killed a couple of them. I never paid much attention to that crap. For all I care, they could've blown up the whole bunch of them and the world would've been a better place."

"Randy! That's not a very Christian thing to say."

Mischke wrinkled his nose. "There's nothing Christian about poisoning people with drugs."

I laid the ring picture on the table. "Have either of you ever seen someone wearing a ring that looks like this?"

They both shook their heads. "It's not familiar," Randy said. "Sorry to run, but I've got work backed up out the door and an oil furnace that just blew up."

We stood, but Peggy protested. "Finish your coffee and have a cookie."

I was ready to walk out, but Jill put her hand on my arm. "Finish your coffee."

Queenie moved to Jill's thigh when we sat down. Jill petted the dog and sipped her coffee. "How long have you lived here?"

"Better than fifty years now. We moved to the Falls right after we got married. Randy had a job at the paper mill back then. He was working all kinds of overtime, and I'd just had our first son. One day, he came home and said the guy who built repair parts for the mill was retiring. Randy talked to the bank, and they gave us a mortgage for the house and the machine shop. He quit at the mill and has been working seven days a week since."

"That sounds like my dad's ranch," Jill said, hoping to keep Peggy talking. "Taking care of animals is a 24/7 job."

"Randy talked about guiding fishermen. It paid better than the machine shop, but he got fed up with the entitled and unhappy idiots. Sometimes the fish just don't bite. And sometimes a storm comes up, and you shouldn't be on the water."

"We heard that Randy's boat blew away in a storm. The anchor was missing when it was found."

That comment seemed to jar Peggy. "That's when it was. Yes! The big June storm that knocked down all those trees. Randy and the neighbors spent a week cutting down trees that were blocking the road and on people's roofs. One of our neighbors found

Randy's boat and towed it back here. It had washed up on the rocks, and something broke in the motor."

"Do you remember anything else about that time? Was there anything going on with the neighbors?"

"With cabin people for neighbors, there's always something going on. You know how it goes. Someone's son is a troublemaker. Someone's daughter is flirting with the boys in town. Somebody's motor dies, and the rest of the guys go out to look for him."

"Think about that time, in the late '80s. Was there anything going on that made you uneasy or concerned about what was happening?"

"Like I said, I was busy raising kids. I didn't notice too much about what was happening in town unless it was school-related." Seeing that we hadn't touched the Oreos, Peggy pulled the package open and slid it to Everett. "A young guy like you needs to keep his energy up."

"Thanks, ma'am. I didn't want to be the only one eating your cookies."

"Yeah, Everett, you need your energy to keep up with that new girlfriend who works at Davidson's," I kidded.

Peggy stopped with an Oreo suspended over her cup. "There was something about a girl who worked at the resort." She dunked her cookie while she thought. "No, it was a guy working at the resort who was dating one of the cabin people's daughters. They got caught doing something, probably what young people do in the backseat of a car. Her parents shipped her home and he..."

"He, what?" Jill asked.

"I think he got fired. It's hard to say because we really didn't have anything to do with the resort people unless they needed an outboard motor repaired."

"Do you remember any of their names?"

Peggy shook her head. "There have been a couple dozen folks who owned cabins near here over the years. Some stay around for decades; others decide the drive is too long or the fishing isn't as good as they'd hoped. Sometimes the wives get tired of cleaning and taking care of the kids while the guys fish and drink."

"Have you ever had problems with burglaries or vandalism?" I asked.

"Not down here at the end of the road. I think some of the cabins were broken into one year, but no one bothers us."

"Does Randy run the business all by himself?" I asked.

Peggy rolled her eyes. "He's getting too old to keep doing this much longer. Every year, he gets busier, and people want their repairs done faster."

"Has he ever had a helper?"

"There have been several over the years. Because we really only need two people during the summer, most guys work with Randy for a few months, then move on.

Either that, or they think there's an easier way to make money than getting greasy, working long hours, and lifting heavy stuff. Young people want to make big bucks without having to break a sweat."

"Was anyone working here in the '80s when the boat drifted away?"

Peggy tapped the table with her fingertip. "There was a Dwayne something, a smart kid. Randy liked him a lot, but he was kind of bookish. I think he went to a tech school somewhere that following fall." Peggy frowned, then nodded. "He actually worked a couple of summers for us while he was off school."

"Do you have his name written down somewhere?" Jill asked.

Peggy looked tired. "I suppose it's somewhere in our tax stuff. We paid him, so we must have some Social Security and income tax payment records. The Lord only knows where Randy would have that stuff, unless he burned it."

"Did Randy use an accountant or bookkeeper who might have the records?"

"Check with April Perrine in I-Falls. She's done our taxes for years."

Jill bent down and ruffled Queenie's ears before standing to shake Peggy's hand. Outside, we found the furnace repair truck parked alongside our Park Service pickup truck. I walked into the shop where I found Randy and the furnace guy dismantling the old furnace.

"Randy, would April Perrine have your records from when Dwayne worked for you?"

"Yeah, I suppose she might. I don't know how many years she keeps income tax files. I think the government only requires you to keep them for seven years."

We sat idling outside the machine shop while Everett swatted mosquitoes. When he felt he'd killed enough, he returned down the road. He glanced at me. "What do you think about the guy from the resort dating the girl from a cabin?"

"It seems plausible. Maybe even probable. A summer romance."

"It seems pretty extreme for Mom and Dad to pack her up and take her back home."

"Maybe it was more than just a teen romance."

"There are a lot of possible scenarios," Jill interjected. "Maybe her parents caught them naked in the back seat of a car. Maybe her parents thought he was too old for her. Maybe she got pregnant."

Everett became very quiet as we drove. "Do you have any theories?" I asked.

My question pulled him back from his daydreaming. "Um, no. I was just thinking about...other stuff."

Reading into what *stuff* might be, I asked, "What's up between you and Laney?"

"It's yet to be determined."

"That's a vague non-answer," Jill observed.

"We're getting serious. I've been more serious than she is, because she's got a boyfriend back in Mankato."

"Something changed last night?"

"I guess so."

"You don't seem sure," I observed.

He glanced at me and asked, "When did you two know you were in love? I mean, really in love."

I turned to Jill. "This is your question."

"Why is it mine? You were the one..." she paused. "Oh, the one-night stand."

Everett frowned. "The one-night stand?"

"We were working together, and Doug had accepted a job at a different park. He said he had feelings for me. I told him he was leaving, and I wasn't into one-night stands."

"What happened?"

"I had a long, introspective conversation with myself and decided whatever happened that night was not going to be a one-night stand. I moved to his new post with him, and six months later, we were married."

"Is that how you saw it, Doug?"

I glanced at Jill. "Not entirely. I knew Jill was balking because of my upcoming move. When she knocked on the door, I was prepared to make popcorn and watch an old movie, because I knew she wasn't interested in a one-night stand. At some point in the evening, I realized we were going to be together."

"Be together forever?"

"Yes, I believed that."

"You guys were adults then, right? Laney is going to be a college junior next year."

Jill reached over the seat and put her hand on Everett's shoulder. "She's an adult, Ev. This could be the great love of your life. Why not see if it is?"

"Her dad might kill me if she quits college."

"Even if she decides to hang around up here, she doesn't have to quit college," I suggested. "She can transfer her credits. I saw a community college in town. There are two colleges in Duluth, one in Bemidji, and another in Superior. They're all closer than Mankato."

Everett turned toward International Falls and drove in silence. As we neared town, he glanced at me. "We need to know more about this dead guy from the motel and his girlfriends. That sounds really messed up. I could see the angry father of a teenage daughter doing something violent. I mean, if she was underage and got pregnant..."

"There are a lot of things an angry father might've done far short of killing the guy and dumping his body in the lake," Jill reasoned.

Everett looked at Jill in the mirror. "I've got a fourteen-year-old sister. If some older guy knocked her up, my dad would kill him."

"Maybe it wasn't a guy working at one of the resorts. What if it was Mischke's helper?"

"Or, one of the guys cooking meth?" Jill said.

"Laney said she and her roommates are getting invited to parties at someone's cabin or in town every weekend. I don't imagine that's something new."

Jill put her hand on Everett's shoulder again. "Speaking of the resort staff, it might be a good idea if you were prepared for...the evolution of your relationship."

Everett glanced in the mirror. "I...um...think we're okay." After a moment of silence, he added, "You sound like my mom's conscience."

"Think of me as the *good angel* whispering helpful advice."

I chuckled. "As opposed to the *bad angel* on the other shoulder, who's whispering other advice."

Tongue-tied, Everett gave me a sheepish look but nodded.

# Chapter 7

The clouds rolled in as we drove through downtown International Falls. As Megan had predicted, the wind came up, and large raindrops splattered the windshield. Everett found a parking spot just down the street from the accountant's office, and we jogged to her office as the rain became intense.

I'd expected to find a receptionist sitting behind a desk. Instead, we found a gray-haired woman who looked old enough to be my mother, sitting at a library table covered with paper files, a computer keyboard, and a computer monitor. The old storefront's interior walls were lined with file cabinets, a table was surrounded by chairs as if ready for a meeting, and a corner desk had an array of four computer monitors, probably for simultaneous consideration of multiple tax forms. The accountant looked at us with apparent irritation. "Are you lost?"

Jill smiled and walked across the room. "We're Park Service investigators looking into the discovery of the body found in Black Bay. I'm Jill Fletcher."

The woman took off her reading glasses and squinted at Jill, then at Everett and me.

She extended her fingers when Jill tried to shake her hand. "Why are you here?"

"We just spoke with the Mischkes, and they told us you were their accountant."

"And if I am?"

"Peggy Mischke thought you could give us the names of the men who worked for them in the mid-1980s."

"Why would I do that?"

Jill glanced at me, hoping I'd take the lead now that her polite diplomacy had failed.

"We're trying to identify possible suspects in the murder of the person whose body was found with an anchor tied to his foot. It appears Mischke's boat may have been used to deliver the body to its resting place. We need to know who was working for them at the time of the murder so we can evaluate them as suspects."

Perrine sighed, then gestured toward a row of filing cabinets lining the wall farthest from her table. "That information would be somewhere in those file cabinets."

"Are you inviting us to search for the file ourselves?"

After another sigh, Perrine glared at me. "No, I'm trying to explain the herculean effort it might take to glean that one bit of information. I will *NOT* let you dig through those confidential files without a search warrant. I assume you don't have one, or you would've handed it to me when you walked in."

Jill tried to de-escalate the interaction. "We don't have a search warrant because we didn't feel it was necessary. Peggy suggested that we talk with you because she knew your extensive file history might hold the name we need."

The accountant leaned back in her chair, making it squeak. "So, you expect me to drop what I'm doing to dig through 1980s files, hoping I could produce a name for you?"

"The 1989 files might hold our only lead to a murderer."

Perrine's expression softened, and she looked at her watch, then at an open file on the table. "It's nearly noon. Find a café and have lunch. I'll see what I can find in an hour. I'll either have a name by then, or I'll have given up."

Jill smiled and said, "Thank you. We'll see you in an hour."

The intense downpour had passed by the time we left the accountant, leaving behind the slow soaking rain every farmer hoped for. We stood in the sheltered alcove outside the accountant's office. "Where's the nearest café, Everett?"

"The Voyageur Café is around the corner. It's got pretty good food."

I gestured for him to take the lead, and we speed-walked to the café, a one-story building with two picnic tables on the sidewalk outside the entrance. We ducked under the awning and paused by the front door to catch our breath, then we walked in.

About two-thirds of the tables were filled. Everett led us to a back corner table near the kitchen.

"Breakfast all day seems to be their main theme," Jill said as we sat down.

A server burst through the kitchen doors carrying a platter of meals. Everett looked at the selection as she passed. "I had the biscuits and gravy the last time I was here. The biscuits melted in my mouth."

A harried young woman rushed to our table carrying a coffee pot. "Is coffee okay, or would you like something else?"

All three of us flipped up the coffee mugs set on the table. "We'll have coffee. Is there a lunch special?"

The waitress pulled three laminated menus from her apron. "The Voyageur's breakfast is the everyday special. Two eggs, bacon, sausage, and your choice of pancakes, biscuits, or toast."

Everett and I opted for biscuits and gravy. Jill flipped the menu back and forth a couple of times. "I'll have a chef's salad with Italian dressing."

The server had just disappeared into the kitchen when four retirees walked in. Vic waved to us, then left his partners as they claimed a table near the door. "Hey, it's probably good you guys decided not to dive today." He sat in the empty chair at our table, then leaned forward and whispered, "Have you identified the victim yet?"

Everett shook his head. "We're still waiting on DNA from the Duluth ME."

Vic nodded and said, "I've been thinking about this a lot. I don't think Mischke's boat was used to haul the body to Black Bay. There's no way someone would get past his house to steal his boat, then motor back to town, load up a dead body, then motor all the way to Black Bay. It doesn't make any sense."

Trying to act like I appreciated Vic's input, I asked, "So, what boat do you suppose was used for the disposal?"

Vic leaned closer and whispered, "It was a Canadian drug smuggler. I think they go back and forth all the time. They killed this guy, probably because he was skimming profits, and they dumped him in Black Bay to throw us off the trail."

"What about the ring I found?"

Vic leaned back. "That's easy. That skull was a biker thing. Bikers have the biggest drug distribution network. It's linked from Fort Frances to I-Falls. This is a hub for their network."

Everett looked at me to see if I was buying any of Vic's theory. "Wow, Vic. I think you've got it solved. Have you told the sheriff or Border Patrol?"

Vic frowned and shook his head. "I've told them, but they're not interested in solving a 40-year-old cold case. They've got their hands full with cross-border drug smuggling and illegals coming across. Did you hear about the Pakistani family who froze to death walking across the border last winter? One of the border patrol agents found them. They walked in from Canada wearing shorts and flip-flops. Some Canadian coyote took their money and told them to walk across the border to his partner on the other side. They never made it."

"I read about that in my online news feed," Jill said. "It was very sad."

"Yeah, the news people have no idea how many illegal aliens walk across the US/Canadian border a year. They focus on Mexico because of all the people hiking north from Guatemala and El Salvador. They don't give a shit about all the Chinese and Middle Eastern folks who come across here."

Our meals arrived, and Vic stood. "Hey, I'm going back to my guys." He looked at me. "It'd be righteous of you to pick up the tab for our coffee. You've got to look out for your fellow retired law enforcement people."

"Are your buddies retired cops, too?"

Vic glanced at them. "No, but they're with me, and it's my turn to buy."

Jill looked up from her salad. "You're covered, Vic. Enjoy your coffee."

When our server left, Everett whispered, "Vic is always trying to talk someone into buying his coffee."

Jill nodded. "I know. Buying his coffee is the least painful way of getting him to leave."

Everett nodded, then asked as he spread a napkin on his lap, "What do you guys think about his theory that Canadian smugglers disposed of the biker's body?"

Jill actually chuckled. "First of all, I'm not a *guy*. Secondly, we know the ring has an US Army design, not a biker design. Thirdly...Vic is full of shit."

Everett paused and blushed when Jill pointed out that she wasn't a guy. Then he nodded as she made her other points. "You didn't tell him about Mischke's employee."

"Everett, Vic has no need to know anything about our case. He may have been a cop, but now, he's just a nosy civilian who can't keep his mouth shut."

Everett nodded as he chewed his biscuit. "Right. He doesn't have a need to know. But he hears lots of stuff. Doesn't it seem like we should give him a few nuggets that might fit with something he hears somewhere else?"

"We only tell people who need to know. We don't discuss ongoing investigations with anyone outside of active law enforcement."

Jill speared a tomato slice with her fork and waved it at Everett as she spoke. "That 'no discussion of ongoing investigations' includes pillow talk with girlfriends."

Everett's chewing slowed as Jill's admonition hit home. He nodded his understanding and became very focused on his meal.

"How did the Twins do yesterday?" I asked, ending Everett's torment.

"The Twins had a day off after their road trip. The weather guy thought today's home game might be rained out."

* * *

The rain had ended by the time we finished lunch. I don't know if the raindrops actually washed away the mosquitoes or not, but we weren't assaulted by any of the blood suckers as we left the restaurant. April Perrine was back at her library table when we returned at 1:10. She looked up from her computer, then held out a slip of paper. "I found two. Peter Baxter worked for them in '85 and '86. I filed a 1099 for Will Flacowski in '89."

Jill accepted the note and nodded. "Thanks. Does Will Flacowski still live around town?"

"To the best of my knowledge, he never *lived around town*. He stayed in a travel trailer in Mischke's yard for one summer. Then, he moved on. I have no idea what happened to him or where he went."

Perrine turned back to her computer, dismissing us. "Did Flacowski work for Mischkes the entire summer, or only a month or two?"

Perrine's hand remained poised over her keyboard, and she glared at me. "Flacowski's earnings were only $1,874. I surmise that represented only a few weeks of employment, although I didn't see his timecards or checks."

"Thanks for your time," I replied as Perrine returned to her computer without acknowledging me.

Jill looked at the slip of paper. "It's a little spooky that April could look up two names for us and be able to recite the precise wage reported to the IRS."

"Number people are like that. They can pull up telephone numbers and numerical passwords from memory. I bet her fingers fly over the numerical keypad on her computer without glancing down."

Jill looked at the note and recited, "Flacowski made $1,874 in 1989. Baxter made $4,344 in '85 and $4,807 in '86. It appears Mr. Flacowski might've left after six or eight weeks."

"Is there any way to determine if he was Army airborne?" Everett asked, thinking about the ring that had been recovered.

"There is!" I replied as I took out my phone. I looked up the phone number for the Armed Forces record center and punched in their 800 number. After identifying myself and providing my badge number, I asked if they had any records of Will or William Flacowski in the late '70s or early '80s.

We climbed into the pickup while the records center searched. "Investigator Fletcher, I have a William C. Flacowski, who was drafted in 1973 and had an infantry MOS. He served eleven months in Vietnam.

After that, he re-enlisted and went through Airborne school. He spent eleven months in Korea, then went back to Fort Bragg until his discharge in December of 1979."

"Thank you. Do you have a current address for Mr. Flacowski?"

Jill and Everett stared at me as I waited for a response from the records center. "Mr. Flacowski was evaluated for a partial disability by the VA hospital in Minneapolis in 1982. His disability claim, related to Agent Orange exposure, was denied. That's the last information I have on him."

"Is it common for someone to disappear off your records?"

"Anyone who hasn't contacted us about VA benefits, or requested a replacement DD-214, often has an open file without additional information."

"Did Flacowski receive an honorable discharge?"

"No, he received a general discharge."

"Can you see why he wasn't honorably discharged?"

"There's a notation about an arrest and court-martial in Korea."

"What were the charges?"

"He was charged with sexually assaulting a female soldier. It appears the victim separated from the service and failed to appear at the court-martial. The charges were reduced to simple assault, his rank was reduced from Sergeant to PFC, and the case closed."

"Thank you."

Ending the call, I looked at Jill. "William Flacowski was airborne and disappeared from the Army database in 1982. That doesn't mean he's dead. It just means he hasn't been in contact with the VA or Army."

"What's a DD-214?" Everett asked.

"It's the form you get when you're discharged, documenting your separation from the Army. Flacowski has a general discharge, which is less than an honorable discharge, but not as damning as a dishonorable discharge. Because he'd been charged with assaulting a female soldier, but she didn't testify at the court-martial, the charges were reduced. Someone must've reviewed his situation and given him a general discharge."

Jill leaned back. "There are a lot of pieces of the puzzle coming together, and they're pointing at Flacowski."

"Do you have the ME's office on speed dial?" I asked Everett.

"Not speed dial, but they're in my call history." He touched the number, and I gestured for him to hand me his phone.

"Duluth Medical Examiner's office, Paulson speaking."

I explained who I was and my involvement with the John Doe recovered from Rainy Lake. "I just spoke with the Armed Forces record center about a person of interest in our investigation. A lot of the pieces we're turning over suggest that John

Doe is William Flacowski, formerly of the US Army."

"I extracted some DNA from the bones you guys sent us, and I'm running the DNA analysis now. If it's not too badly degraded, I should have something by the end of today. If your guy had been in the Army after 1991, I should be able to compare my results with the records on the DOD DNA database."

"He was a Vietnam vet who was discharged in 1979."

"There was no routine collection of DNA until the Gulf War. At that point, the DOD decided to collect DNA from everyone in case they needed to identify remains."

"Flacowski was charged with sexually assaulting a female soldier. Would the Army collect his DNA when he was charged?"

"I doubt it. However, if his crime was a sexual assault, they might've run a rape kit on the victim and recovered his DNA." Paulson paused. "I bet the prosecutor probably required Flacowski to provide a sample for comparison. I might be able to track something down."

"Do you have contacts in the Department of Defense?"

Paulson laughed. "I've spoken to the people who maintain the DOD DNA data so many times we're on a first-name basis."

"I'm calling from our law enforcement ranger's phone. Let me give you our cell phone numbers."

"What now?" Everett asked.

"Let's go to the sheriff's office. I wonder if Flacowski had an arrest record?"

* * *

The Koochiching County Courthouse complex was located in downtown International Falls. We parked in a spot reserved for law enforcement vehicles. After identifying ourselves to the deputy at the reception desk, we took a seat in the lobby.

"I assume you've been here before," I said to Everett.

"This is where I take people I arrest. It's the nearest detention location."

Jill looked around us at the high ceilings and sandstone block construction. "I never see old buildings like this in use. This is really a showpiece."

The sheriff was holding a door open for us and overheard Jill's comment. "It's a drafty showpiece that's totally inappropriate for today's law enforcement and court security needs. We're building a new center that'll be open in July."

Sheriff "Dutch" Van Horn escorted us to his office, featuring a window overlooking the parking lot. "What can I do for the Park Service?"

"I assume you're aware of the human foot recovered from Black Bay. We're looking into it."

Van Horn nodded and leaned back. "Everett spoke with my deputies. With all of the border stuff going on, I couldn't justify investigating a few bones tied to an anchor. Hell, it could belong to one of the guys who smuggled Canadian whiskey down here during Prohibition."

"We've actually found a possible match with a guy who disappeared in the late 1980s."

Van Horn smiled. "The hell you say! You've made a match based on a few foot bones. Good for you!"

"We also found an arm and a hand with a ring. We think they belong to a guy who worked for Mischke's machine shop. The Duluth ME is trying to match the DNA."

"It sounds like you're making headway. What's your plan?"

"Knowing the time, 1989, and the victim's identity is a step. We'll be tracking down local folks who might remember some old feuds."

"You're convinced the victim didn't die in a boating accident?"

"The anchor was tied to the victim's foot. That wasn't an accident."

Van Horn stood, signaling the end of our conversation. "Let me know if you get something concrete."

* * *


Once out of town, Everett glanced at me. "The sheriff wasn't very excited about our findings."

"That's a double-edged sword. Because he's not interested, there's little pressure on us to produce immediate results. On the other hand, he's not going to help unless we can give him solid evidence of the crime and identify a suspect."

"I'd hoped he would assign someone to assist us."

From the backseat, Jill replied, "Be careful what you wish for. A lot of heat gets put on a case when it appears an arrest is imminent. People leave you alone to plod along in cold cases."

Everett's cell phone rang, and he pulled to the side of the road before answering. He listened for a few moments, nodding and occasionally glancing at me. After ending the call, he said, "That was the Duluth ME's office. The DNA from the bones found with the anchor is badly degraded."

# Chapter 8

Laney waved when she saw us walk in for breakfast the next day. She met us at the table with a coffee pot. "Hi, guys. It sounds like you and Everett were busy yesterday."

"I hope he didn't spill any details about our investigation," I said.

"He doesn't talk about the dead guy. Mostly, he told me how much he's learning from you. As grisly as this sounds, he's really enjoying the investigation." She paused to take out her order pad. "I assume you already know what you're having for breakfast."

After Laney left with our orders, Jill said, "I think it's funny that Everett is enjoying the investigation. He's probably spent his days driving around the park and maybe canoeing the remote lakes alone. This is a big change of pace."

Everett walked into the restaurant and waved. Rather than immediately joining us, he walked to the cash register and spoke to Laney. Her smile was dazzling, and their chemistry was undeniable. She handed him a cup of coffee that he carried to our table.

"Good morning. What's our plan for today?"

"We need to identify and interview some people who were around in 1989. Maybe we can find someone who remembers the victim and has recollections about some triggering event."

Laney arrived with our breakfasts in time to hear my comment about finding past residents. As she set out our plates, she commented, "Your job is recreating ancient history. I mean, you're trying to find people who remember an event that happened before I was born."

Everett nodded. "Ten years before either of us was born."

Laney looked around the restaurant to see if anyone needed her, then said, "I was going to write in the cottage journal about meeting Everett when Megan showed up. We flipped back through the pages and laughed at what some of the girls had written years ago. It's almost like their ghosts are still in the cabin."

"What's the cottage journal?" Jill asked.

"Someone put a notebook on the bookshelf of the seasonal employees' cabin years ago, then wrote a note on the cover that says, 'write your name, the year, your hometown, and a special memory from your time at Davidson's.'"

With my interest piqued, I asked, "What year was the first entry made?"

"Megan and I read the very first entry. Michelle Weyer wrote about a bat flying around inside the cabin in 1961. We laughed because that would've freaked us out, too."

"Are there entries from every year?" Jill asked.

"I don't know if someone wrote *every* year. There are names and entries from every decade. I mean, like a hundred people wrote something. It's a time capsule."

"Could we look at it?" I asked.

"I don't know why not. Do you want me to get it now?"

A customer waved to get Laney's attention. "Take care of your other customers. If you don't get a break, we can walk to the cabin and look at it."

"No visitors are allowed in the cabins. The four of us work different shifts, so it seems like someone is always trying to sleep or is running to the bathroom in her underwear. I'll retrieve it for you when I get a second."

As Laney walked away, Everett added, "She makes me wait for her on the steps or in the pickup. I've never seen inside their cabin except what's visible when she opens the door." He leaned close so he couldn't be overheard. "They're...slobs. I mean, there are clothes and stuff strewn around. I think that's the real reason they don't want anyone inside."

Jill chuckled. "I remember living in park service housing with other women.

Bathroom time was always an issue, as was entertaining male guests. About ninety percent of our arguments were about those two things."

"What were the other ten percent?" I asked.

Jill thought for a second. "Food. We each bought our own groceries, and it seemed like someone would always lose track of how many yogurts they'd eaten and help themselves to whatever was in the refrigerator."

"Huh," I replied. "I would've guessed who washed dishes was a big issue."

Everett shook his head. "Nah, you just leave a pile of dirty dishes on the counter, and then you wash the one plate and fork you need to eat your meal. It's that way until someone's mother shows up, is disgusted, and then she washes the whole mess."

Jill shuddered. "The women wouldn't tolerate that. We'd let the dishes accumulate for a day or two. Then, we'd all pitch in and wash the pile."

"It just seems easier to wash them as you use them," I suggested.

Everett frowned at me. "I suppose you're the guy who carries a food wrapper to the wastebasket as soon as you pull it off."

"Why wouldn't you do that?"

Jill patted my arm. "Doug has a bit of cleaning OCD."

"It's not OCD. I've had calls to dump houses. I never want to have someone walk into my house unexpectedly and have to deal with crap and clutter."

Laney rushed by our table. "I'll be back in five. Keep an eye on the cash register."

We'd finished breakfast when Laney rushed in the back door carrying a dog-eared notebook. She left it at the table and rushed away to deal with customers who wanted to settle their bill.

I opened the notebook to the first page and read Mary's entry about the bat, then another about a snake encounter, then passed it to Jill and Everett. He flipped through the pages, then handed it back to me. "It's notes from fifty years of girls picking ticks and talking about cute boys they met."

I opened the book to the 1980s, then flipped to 1989. "Here are notes from the four teens who stayed in the cabin in 1989." The handwriting was terrible, so it took a few minutes for me to decipher the notes. "We know who worked here that year and their hometowns. Carly was homesick and missed her cat. Brenda had 83 wood ticks and lost five pounds because of all the walking. Jackie wrote, 'A Cities *mall maggot* thought I cared about what brand of jeans she wore.'" Seeing a nugget, I read further. "Geezer alert, Biker trying to look twenty is trying to get in everyone's pants. Give me a break!"

I handed the notebook to Jill. "Do you think you can track down Jackie Thomas from Princeton? I think she met our victim."

Jill took out her phone and searched as we waited. "I found Jaqueline Marie Thomas marrying Caden Elliot Benson in Isanti County. The date is June 1992." She went on with her search. "I've got a 1997 telephone listing for Jackie and Caden Benson in St. Francis."

Jill copied and pasted the phone number and put it on speaker. Everett frowned, "Who has a landline anymore?"

"Hello," a woman answered.

"I'm looking for Jackie Thomas Benson."

"Unless you're calling to tell me I've won the Publisher's Clearinghouse grand prize, you can hang up."

"I'm Jill Fletcher, an investigator from the National Park Service. We're looking at a crime in Voyageurs National Park that happened while you worked at Davidson's Resort in 1989."

"Really? That almost sounds like you're real and not a scam."

Chuckling, Jill replied, "I'm very real and I'm not going to ask you for money. We read your notes in Davidson's cottage journal. I'd like to know more about the biker who was hitting on people."

"Davidson's cottage journal?"

"It's the notebook left in the cabin where you lived that summer. Everyone wrote their name, hometown, and some memories from their summer. Do you remember that?"

"Phew! Sorry, I have to switch mental gears."

"Did anything exciting happen that summer? You shared the cabin with Carly, Mary, and Brenda," Jill added, hoping the names would trigger memories.

"I remember being swarmed by mosquitoes and picking ticks off myself. There was always tension because of four girls sharing a bathroom." Jackie paused, and Jill let the silence hang. "THE SNAKE!" Jackie blurted out. "The biggest event of the summer was when Mary stepped on the snake. It was epic! She was oblivious, always lost in her thoughts when she walked around. There was a garter snake on the cabin path, and she didn't see it until she stepped on it. I swear she peed her pants."

"It's amazing how a little event like that can stick in your mind," Jill suggested. "You made a note about a biker who was trying to look young and hitting on the women. Can you recall anything about him?"

"It's funny. I have few memories about so much of my life. That summer was so unusual, compared to anything I'd experienced until then. I suppose those intensely different experiences etched themselves in my brain." She paused again. "I dropped a tray of food coming out of the lodge kitchen. I thought the cook or Mr. Davidson would kill or fire me. The cook was disgusted, but she helped me pick up the pieces, then cooked up a replacement meal. Mr. Davidson was...incredible. He took me aside. I thought he was going to scream at me. Instead, he sat me down and told me to take a breath. It's like the kindest thing a boss has ever done. He said the plates were replaceable. The mess was cleaned up. Then, he told me to take a deep breath and go on with my job. You know that advice has stuck with me. I've never yelled at a co-worker because of a mistake."

"Think about the biker," Jill said, trying to redirect the discussion.

"I can picture him. Um, Bill? Will? He came around on Friday nights when all of the vacationers were winding down as they prepared to leave on Saturday morning. He'd talk to the fishermen but always bought a drink for any woman sitting alone at the bar. The way he acted was...creepy. It still gives me chills thinking about his arm around some drunk woman's shoulder."

"Did he ever hit on you or any of the underage girls at the restaurant?"

"Oh, wow. You're digging deep into forgotten memories. He never hit on me. He liked blondes, and I have mousy brown hair. I think the cook warned us to stay clear of him." Jackie paused, then spouted, "Oh! Mr. Davidson threw him out one night. He was talking to the daughter of a guest, and Mr. Davidson peeled him off the girl and took him outside. I don't know what was said, but I heard the motorcycle engine start, and he raced away. Mr. Davidson came back inside and spoke to the girl, who seemed embarrassed."

"Did you see Will Flacowski after that?"

"That's it. Someone called him Flaco the Fake-O. I guess he had stories about everything."

"Did you ever see him giving a motorcycle ride to a girl?"

"I can't imagine anyone getting on his bike. I mean, he was something else. It would've been like my father's friends hitting on me. Yuck."

"Were any of the other girls in the cabin blonde? Did Flacowski hit on them?"

"Mary was blonde. I don't recall her being approached by Flaco. On the other hand, I worked in the restaurant, and Mary worked in housekeeping. Our work didn't cross over much. Although, I don't know why someone in housekeeping would interact with someone who wasn't a resort guest."

"Do you stay in touch with the other girls from that summer?"

"We said we'd stay in touch. That never happened. I have no idea where any of them are these days."

Jill gave Jackie her phone number and asked her to call if she remembered anything more about Will Flacowski or his interaction with other people at the resort or in town. After ending the call, she looked at me. "She remembered Flacowski and had a good grasp of what he was like. It's interesting that Mr. Davidson threw Flacowski out of the lodge when he hit on a vacationer's daughter."

"Flaco the Fake-O," I repeated. "That says so much about what people thought of him."

Jill went back to her phone and started entering information. After a few minutes, she said, "I can't find phone numbers, Minnesota marriage certificates, criminal records, death certificates, or driver's licenses for the other three names. I assume they moved out of state."

Everett cocked his head. "I had a friend who got married on a cruise ship. They wanted to have a drunken reception and reasoned that none of the wedding party or attendees would get a DUI on the drive home if they partied on the ship. I wonder how that was recorded?"

"Did any of the drunks fall overboard?" Jill asked.

"I didn't go. A big drunken party on a ship isn't my scene." As he stood, Everett asked, "What's our plan for today?"

"Jill's going to call Rachel to see when she's available to dive with us again. Aside from that, I'd like to knock on doors on the road to Mischke's machine shop. I hope one of the owners was around in 1989."

Rachel answered quickly. Whatever she said made Jill laugh and glance at me. "I'm entirely warmed up, thank you." She listened for a few more seconds, then nodded. "I think this afternoon, about two o'clock, would work."

I looked at Everett and asked, "Can you knock on doors without us while we go diving with Rachel?"

"No problem. If you need doors knocked on, I'm your man."

Jill nodded and confirmed our dive appointment with Rachel. "She's off at one o'clock. She said she'll have the boat ready, the gear loaded, and will check with Lance and Parker, but assumes they're working. There's another diver who might be available too. If he's free, she'll invite him along."

Everett turned onto Mischke's road and drove into the first driveway. The cabin wasn't visible from the road. As we drove down the muddy pot-holed ruts, a very rustic cabin appeared through the trees.

"Wow," Jill commented from the back seat, "that reminds me of some ranch houses in the Black Hills. The original homesteaders built a one-room shack, then added a room every time they had another kid."

"Yeah, it looks like there are about five different rooflines on this building. It appears most of the siding is actually rolled roofing, and there are only three tiny windows."

"Windows were expensive. You only put in enough to let in a little light and to allow some cross ventilation in the summer."

The area immediately around the cabin had been recently mown, and a lawnmower was visible in a backyard shed not far from the cabin. A small square building, probably once an outhouse, was the structure farthest from the cabin.

The door opened, and a giant black and brown mongrel trudged out and sat on the single concrete step, acting as though racing out to check on us would be too great an effort. A moment later, a man dressed in bib overalls and a quilted long underwear shirt stepped out. If not for his recently trimmed white hair and neat beard, I would've assumed he was a hermit. He cocked his head as if we were a curiosity.

I stepped out of the pickup and waved. "Good morning." I waited with one foot still inside the pickup to see if the dog was going to react aggressively to my exit. Rather than showing aggression, the dog flopped down with a grunt.

"I don't recall ever seeing a Park Service pickup down here," the man said.

"We're investigating the body found across the bay."

The man nodded toward the cabin. "Get yourselves in here before the mosquitoes discover there's fresh blood available."

"What about the dog?" I asked as I approached the house.

"Just step over Shemp."

"Shemp?" Jill asked as she followed me into the cabin's small kitchen.

The man chuckled. "Larry, Moe, and Curly are buried by the outhouse. Since Shemp was the last of the Three Stooges, this dog might have to be the last."

Four rustic chairs with thatched seats sat around an equally rustic-looking table. The cupboards were old, but well-maintained and free of clutter. A newer refrigerator and stove took up one wall of the small kitchen. The man popped a pod into a coffee maker and started a hissing cycle. "If you're willing to drink Keurig, I can whip up coffee quickly."

"I'd take a cup," I replied. Jill also accepted. Everett shook his head.

"Your view of the lake is incredible," Jill said, looking through the arch between the kitchen and living rooms.

The man chuckled as he carried a steaming mug to Jill. "I put my money into the interior of the cabin and the lakeside windows. I like to believe that a thief driving in will see the ramshackle outside toward the road and assume it won't be worth his time to break in." Setting the cup down, he nodded at me. "I'm Stan Bauer."

We made introductions as Stan returned to retrieve another mug from the coffee maker. "Do you know anything about the foot that was tied to an anchor?" I asked.

"If you're asking if I'm responsible, the answer is no. If you're asking if I'd heard the news that the anchor murder foot had been found, yes."

With two mugs in his hands, Stan sat down across from me. "What else can I tell you?"

"Do you know who the victim was?"

A smile flickered on Bauer's lips. "Vic English has told everyone in I-Falls that the victim is a druggie from the 1980s who was killed at the motel, then dragged to the lake." When I didn't answer immediately, Stan smiled. "I figured that was probably fiction."

"How long have you owned this cabin?"

"My grandfather built it in the early 1900s. Grandpa was a logger, and this was his summer place. He spent winters living in the logging camps."

"We think the victim died in 1989, possibly during a storm."

Bauer nodded. "My brother helped Randy Mischke look for his boat after the big blow. Vic said it was Randy's anchor tied to the foot you found."

Without confirming or denying anything, I asked, "Who do you think the victim was?"

Bauer leaned back and rested his coffee cup on his considerable belly. "Well, if you'd asked me that in 1989, I would've said it was probably one of the local meth heads who'd overdosed, and his buddies dumped his body."

"Do you have a different thought about the identity now?"

"When I signed my taxes yesterday, April Perrine said you'd been asking about one of Mischke's deadbeat employees."

Jill shook her head. "You've got to love a small town."

"Don't worry about April spreading the news. She's tight-lipped about her clients."

"But she told you," I countered.

"April is my sister-in-law. I'm the one person in town she can talk to. Everyone else gets credibility among the rumor crowd by passing on everything they hear."

"You don't?"

"I worked for a federal government agency known for keeping secrets. I don't share anything with anyone."

"Which agency?" I asked.

"You don't have a need to know."

I noticed a blinking light under the cupboard, and a glow emanated from another cupboard where the door was ajar. "It appears you have quite a security system here."

He reached over and closed the cupboard door, hiding the electronics. "I dislike surprises."

"I apologize if we've surprised you."

"I've been expecting you since yesterday. Dutch called and said he thought you'd stop by."

"You and the sheriff..."

"Have common interests. He looks out for me and my place. I sometimes supply him with information pertinent to things happening along the border."

Everett frowned. "I've been here almost twenty months, and I've never heard of you before we drove down your driveway."

"And that's how I prefer things. If you hadn't been in law enforcement, your arrival would've been less cordial, and there would've been a county deputy parked behind your pickup by now."

Bauer shifted in his chair as if his leg was cramping. I caught a glimpse of the butt of a very large pistol under his overalls. "Tell us about the night before Mischke's boat disappeared."

"There's not much to tell. There was a hell of a big storm. Lightning. Thunder. Heavy winds blew down our power lines."

"Did you hear or see anything unusual?"

"Like a guy screaming as someone tied an anchor to him and dumped him overboard? No, I didn't hear that."

"How about unusual traffic on the road? Someone with a body in their trunk driving past to steal Mischke's boat."

"I can't hear anything less than a concrete truck driving down the road, and as you know, the road isn't visible from my house."

"How about a motorcycle passing by?" Jill asked. "One of Mischke's employees had a motorcycle."

The tiniest bit of annoyance registered on Bauer's face. "Flacowski."

"I take it you didn't like Flacowski?" I asked.

"You'd be hard pressed to find someone who *liked* Flacowski."

"Did you tell Randy Mischke that?"

Bauer shifted again and rubbed his left leg. "As I said, I'm a very private person. I don't interact much with the neighbors. I try to be socially invisible."

"But you knew Flacowski's name?"

Bauer leaned forward and set his mug on the table. "Mr. Flacowski was a bit of an issue."

"Please explain what that means."

Bauer paused while composing his response. At that moment, he reminded me of a lawyer who'd been called to testify in a trial. He didn't want to be on the witness stand and didn't want to be led into the answers the county attorney expected him to give. It was somewhat like watching a chess match. Fun to watch. Not fun to be the one playing it.

"Mr. Flacowski came to my attention due to some of his activities unrelated to his employment at Mischke's machine shop."

"Some illegal activities?" I asked.

"There was suspicion that his arrival here coincided with some other illegal activities."

"Did those other illegal activities factor into his death?"

"I don't know how, why, or under what circumstances he died. As far as I knew, he'd disappeared."

"Did you report his disappearance?"

"It was irrelevant to me."

"Do you know who had a motive to kill him?"

"Not knowing what he did…"

I stopped Bauer. "We're in the middle of a murder investigation. I don't have time for riddles or misdirection. What was Flacowski into?"

"I suspect, but can't prove, that he was involved in moving drugs through the area. He'd shown up at some places where innocent people don't go, at times when innocent people are in bed."

"We heard he may have had some encounters with some women in the area."

"I can't comment on any of his sexual conquests."

"Can't, or won't?"

"From my standpoint, those are the same thing."

"You are aware of a Flacowski 'sexual conquest' that complicated your observation of his activities."

"It didn't impact my…"

"Nod or shake your head. Did Flacowski rape someone?"

Bauer shrugged. "I have no direct knowledge or evidence about his involvement in a sexual assault."

"You have suspicions. Who was the victim?"

"I don't know."

"Do you think someone associated with the victim killed Flacowski?"

"That's a possible scenario. There's also a chance that his death was totally unrelated to his disgusting…"

"Disgusting, what?" Jill asked.

"The whole group of meth people had the morals of alley cats. Flacowski fit right in with them. I won't say anything more about the subject."

"Do you think one of them killed him?" I asked.

"To be honest, the meth cooking people didn't have..." Bauer paused. "No, I don't think they killed him. Someone further up the meth supply chain might've had a problem with Will, but not the meth *cooking* bunch."

"Let me guess. You're still watching the supply chain?"

"What's the phrase used on the cop shows? Our inquiries are ongoing." Bauer stood, signaling the end of the discussion. "I assume you don't need to be told that what I've said, and implied, is not attributable to me. I will not testify in court. Don't return to clarify any questions you have."

"You won't answer the door?" I asked as we walked out of the house and stepped over Shemp.

"I'll be indisposed." Bauer slapped his thigh. "C'mon, dog. Get inside before the mosquitoes suck you dry."

"What did we learn from that?" Everett asked as he turned the pickup around in the yard.

"Flacowski was into something drug-related. If it was the drug people who killed him, it wasn't the local crew. We also learned that Flacowski had the morals of an alley cat and was involved in something sexual that wasn't reported to the police."

"Who do you think that guy works for?" Jill asked.

"We're close to the border. I'd say he's either a DEA agent or he's with Customs and Border Protection."

"He's undercover in his grandparents' cabin?" Everett asked.

"It's a great cover story," I replied. "I doubt much of it is true. As for his relatives who've stayed at the cabin, I doubt he has a DNA connection with any of the past residents."

Everett turned his head toward me and frowned. "What?"

"Did you notice his slight Canadian accent? His 'about' sounded more like 'aboot.'"

From the back seat, Jill added, "Ignore Doug's paranoia."

"I'll offer you a bet," I replied. "If we find any of the other neighbors at home, they'll recall that family cabin being occupied by a string of children and cousins of the original owners."

"I don't get it," Everett replied.

"There was surveillance equipment in the cupboards and who knows what else hidden in the other rooms with closed doors. I think Mr. Bauer works for the RCMP and is running a parallel operation with the US

Customs and Border Protection to catch smugglers and drug runners."

"But he knew about Flacowski!" Everett protested.

"Have you ever heard the term *institutional knowledge*? It's what a good undercover operative has as part of his backstory. There's a whole package of information you memorize so you're credible."

# Chapter 9

Everett turned into a driveway on the opposite side of the road and navigated an equally narrow, muddy driveway. The underbrush had been cut back, and more of the yard was mown, giving this cabin a park-like feel. A wooden kiddy castle with swings and a slide was built alongside the cabin and a bicycle leaned against a garage. A golden retriever woofed at us as we approached. His ears perked up and his tail wagged, so I took his bark as more of a greeting than a threat.

A woman opened the screen door, and the dog rushed inside, peeking at us around the woman's legs as we approached. "Some guard dog," Jill whispered.

"Can I help you?" the woman asked as she stepped outside and closed the door behind herself. She was trim, possibly forty years old, wearing jeans and a maroon Minnesota Gophers sweatshirt.

I introduced us and learned she was Jessica Carpenter. She didn't invite us in. "We're investigating the anchor murder, as the newspaper has called it."

"That's terrible. I'm so glad the bones were found in Black Bay, on the other side of this peninsula."

"How long have you owned this cabin?" I asked.

"I suppose twelve years. Our kids were toddlers when we bought it. Now, they're teens." She glanced at the door. "I'd invite you in, but I think they're all asleep. They all turned nocturnal once they hit their adolescence."

"Did you meet the previous owners?"

Jessica shook her head. "We purchased it from an estate. I understood an older couple had owned it for years. Their kids decided to sell it after the parents passed away."

"Do you know their names?"

"I'm sure it's on the purchase agreement but all that paperwork is stored at our home in St. Cloud. A realtor in town handled the sale. I'm sure he could tell you who the past owners were."

"Do you remember which realtor?" I asked.

The woman chuckled. "His smiling face is on every restaurant placemat and billboard in I-Falls."

A voice called from inside the cabin, "Mom, do we have any orange juice?"

"Look in the refrigerator." The woman shook her head. "Like I would store orange juice anywhere else."

"Mom, Jayce ate the last granola bar!"

"There are more in the cupboard by the cereal."

"Which cupboard?"

The woman tipped her head back as if overwhelmed by the question. "The one with the cereal, next to the microwave."

"Instant oatmeal sounds good. Do we have any?"

"In the cupboard with the cereal and granola bars." The woman looked at us and shook her head. "I think the ability to reason is lost when their hormones start to flow."

I chuckled. "Thanks for your time."

I turned toward the truck when Jill asked, "Have you met Mr. Bauer, across the road?"

"I see an old pickup come and go. We wave, but I've never spoken to the man or his wife."

"He's married?" Jill asked.

"I assume he is. I saw a woman driving the pickup the first couple of years we were here. I've only seen the husband lately."

"Thanks," Jill said before falling in step beside me. Once the woman had stepped inside Jill said, "Bauer didn't say anything about a wife and the decorating didn't look like it had been done by a woman."

"The Bauers haven't been seen together. I assume that means there was a change of operatives."

Everett shook his head. "Or his wife divorced him because she couldn't stand living in a rustic cabin in the boonies."

The next cabin's driveway was overgrown with weeds, and their dock was stacked next to the building, which indicated to me that the owners probably came up later in the summer when the weather was more pleasant. A man's voice came through a speaker built into the doorbell as we approached the door. "Can I help you?"

"We're investigating the anchor murder. We'd like to ask you a few questions."

"Please hold your badge up to the camera."

I unclipped my badge and held it a few inches from the camera built into the doorbell as I swatted at the mosquitoes that swarmed out of the front door's alcove when I approached.

"Thank you. We're not actually at the cottage now. The doorbell senses when someone approaches and cameras give me a live feed through the Wi-Fi." Solheim explained that they lived in Fergus Falls and only went up to their cottage on long weekends and for two weeks each summer. They'd purchased the lot with a dilapidated cabin they razed in 2003. He didn't know who the previous owners had been.

"Have you met any of the neighbors?"

"I've met a few of them. Randy Mischke fixed my outboard motor and welded a couple of dock brackets for me. The Carpenters are nice folks and our kids used to play together when they were younger. I met Connie Bauer when we first moved in. She's kind of reclusive. I saw her on the road once in a while, but there's been a guy staying there for the last couple of years. I don't know if she sold the property or if that's her husband or brother."

"Thanks Mr. Solheim."

Jill and Everett were already walking to the pickup, seeking refuge from the mosquitoes, when Solheim said, "Tell me more about this anchor murder. Is it something we should be concerned about?"

"It's a cold case from 1989. We know very little except that some bones were found in Black Bay with an anchor."

"Nothing recent, then?"

"No. We're relatively certain the death occurred in 1989."

"Thanks. It appears the mosquitoes are attacking. You should get into your pickup."

As we pulled out of that driveway, Jill said, "He'd met Connie Bauer, who hasn't been seen in a few years. Maybe we should go back and question Stan about his missing female relative."

"Stan has a story that will withstand scrutiny. I don't see any point in pushing him on it. If we did, I suspect we'd receive a call from Jack asking us to step away from the Bauers, without any specifics besides our lack of a need to know. That's the universal signal that you're sniffing around another agency's undercover operation and further interference might jeopardize it." When Jill didn't reply, I added, "There's nothing worse than having another agency come poking around your sting or surveillance operation while you're trying to remain incognito. Most often, the local police are aware of the operation and have been asked to stay clear."

"Ah," Everett said. "The sheriff probably knows about it."

"You can bet Van Horn is keeping his people away from Bauer's driveway."

The next cabin was also empty, although the driveway weeds were crushed, indicating someone had been there before us. I suggested returning to Mischke's as Everett pulled out of the final driveway on the peninsula. Jill's phone rang as we drove into Mischke's yard.

"Hi, Jack," was all the conversation I heard until she replied, "we will comply."

I turned to Jill and said, "Jack says we should stay clear of Bauer's cabin."

She nodded as she ended the call. "I guess you win the bet."

Mischke's shop was empty. Peggy opened the door before we knocked. "Got time for a cup of coffee?" she asked, holding the door open. "Get in here before the mosquitoes carry you away."

Randy Mischke was making a sandwich on the counter. He nodded and said, "Anyone hungry? I'm a whiz at bologna and Velveeta sandwiches."

"No thanks," I replied.

Peggy gestured toward the kitchen chairs and took coffee mugs from the cupboard. "You're missing out on the one thing Randy 'cooks.'"

"I haven't had a Velveeta sandwich since I was a kid," Jill replied.

"This is your big chance!" Randy said, holding up the log of cheese.

Jill raised her hand, making a stop gesture. "I wasn't that taken with Velveeta when I was eight. It's an acquired taste, and it's long gone."

Peggy delivered steaming cups of coffee to the table. "I can't stomach Velveeta. The doctor told me to cut back on cholesterol and salt. I think those are the first two Velveeta ingredients."

Randy picked up the box and read the label. "Nope, the first ingredient is cheese."

Chuckling, Jill asked, "Is the second ingredient plastic to give it that special texture?"

"Nope. Plastic is not listed."

Peggy ended the Velveeta discussion by sitting and asking, "What can we do for you today?"

"Can you tell us anything more about Flacowski's departure?"

Peggy shook her head. "One day he didn't show up for work. He wasn't in the trailer either."

Randy pulled a package of Oreos from the cupboard, peeled back the lid, and set them on the table. "Help yourselves." He took a huge bite from his sandwich and pulled several Oreos from the package.

Everett took two cookies and Peggy handed each of us a paper napkin.

"Do you have anything to add to Peggy's recollection of Flacowski's disappearance?" I asked.

"Nope. I was swamped with work and that lazy sonofabitch didn't even have the courtesy to tell me he was quitting. I always figured you owed your bosses at least two-weeks' notice when you were planning to leave. I guess that's just not a thing with young people anymore."

"That was forty years ago," Jill said. "And Flacowski wasn't that young."

Randy waved off Jill's comments. "He acted like a stupid teenager. He had no work ethic. He'd see the clock getting close to quitting time, and he'd wipe his hands and walk away. I tell you, he didn't finish the job or put the tools away. He'd just walk off, leaving everything just sitting there. It wasn't right. You always finish what you're doing, even if it takes an extra half hour or more. And you put away the tools so you can find them the next time you do something. Every machinist takes care of his tools. That's how we make a living. You take care of your tools, and they take care of you."

Peggy stared at her coffee. "Randy spends a lot of time teaching the young people we hire. They either learn to do things correctly, take care of the tools, and clean up after themselves, or he fires them."

"Why did you put up with Flacowski?" I asked.

"I was young, swamped, there weren't any experienced people available, and Flacowski was slightly better than working alone. Slightly."

"Do you remember him after all these years?" I asked.

Peggy nodded while Randy ate. "We remember the really good helpers and the really bad ones. Flacowski was part of that bad group."

"Where did you send his last check?" Jill asked.

Peggy looked at Randy. "I don't recall. He never left a forwarding address."

"I don't think there was a check. I paid every Friday, and he left partway through the week."

"Didn't he have an emergency contact or..."

Randy cut Jill off. "Flacowski was a homeless vet. I fell for his hard luck story and borrowed a trailer for him to live in. We didn't know anything about his past except his stupid stories about the Army."

"You didn't know he had a *less than honorable* Army discharge?" I asked.

"Really?" Randy asked. "According to Flacowski, he'd been screwed out of receiving a medal of honor."

"We did some research. He was sent home from Korea after some legal problems. The Army shoved him out of the door with a general discharge."

Randy blew out a breath. "That explains a lot, including why he was reluctant to contact the VA about being screwed over."

"We asked your neighbors about their memory of Flacowski. Most of them moved here after 1989."

"Yeah," Randy agreed. "Bauers are probably the only ones who owned back then, and the parents are dead."

"Is there anyone else from that era nearby?"

"There's a Christmas tree farm on the way here from town. The Dupre family has owned that land forever," Randy suggested. He looked at Peggy as if hoping she'd remember someone else. "The Davidsons' have owned the resort forever. Their staff turns over, but family members have always gone to school in town."

Peggy's face lit up. "Talk to Lyle Sertich!"

Randy snorted. "If you can catch him when he's sober."

"Randy, cut him some slack," Peggy protested. "Lyle was the star hockey player. He was the starting center for the Broncos when they won the '65 and '66 state hockey tournaments. If he hadn't been drafted, he'd probably have made a pro team."

Jill frowned. "Who are the Broncos? That sounds like a South Dakota team."

Randy smiled and looked at me. "Doug, you're a Minnesota kid. Do you know the answer?"

"I bet they're named after Bronco Nagurski, who was an NFL Hall of Fame player from International Falls."

Randy puffed up. "Darn straight. Helluva big guy. He was discovered by a University of Minnesota football scout who found him pulling a plow like an ox."

"I think that's a myth," I replied.

Peggy interrupted the banter. "Lyle Sertich worked for Davidson's after he came back from the Army. He'd know a lot of the people around town."

After succumbing to the call of the Oreos, I thanked Randy and Peggy. At the door, I asked, "What did Flacowski do when he wasn't working? Do you know where he hung out?"

Peggy got a sly smile. "It wasn't the Lutheran church."

Randy laughed. "Will was more of a drinking and swearing guy."

"Did he mention any particular bar as his favorite?" I asked.

"The bar owners turn over every few years, and the names change. He said something about the Blind Pig Tap once, but that might've been because they'd thrown him out."

"Cal's been the Muni manager since he turned twenty-one. He might remember Flacowski," Peggy added.

"The Muni?" Jill asked.

"The municipal bar and liquor store is kind of the center of one social hub."

"Or you could just start at one end of town and stop at every bar along the way. I imagine that's what Flacowski did until he found a place and patrons who'd put up with his line of bullshit," Randy suggested.

I looked at Everett. "How many bars have you been in?"

The question caught him off guard. "I'm not much of a bar guy. I've been to a couple of them. There are like a dozen others."

Jill frowned. "A dozen bars in a town the size of I-Falls?"

Randy laughed. "The winters here are long, cold, and lonely."

"It's sometimes fun to drive into town for a beer just to see who's around and what's new." Peggy nudged Randy's elbow. "Not that Randy's not good company. It's just nice to talk to someone else once in a while."

# Chapter 10

We ate lunch at a pizza place on the outskirts of I-Falls and talked about the unlikely odds of finding anyone who remembered a guy who called himself Will Flaco or Flacowski hanging around a bar in town. Everett seemed pleased by that consensus. "I didn't want to hit all of the bars in town. Nobody in a bar wants to see a cop walk in."

"You should be a St. Paul cop looking for a suspect in one of the grittier Twin Cities bars. We never went into a bar alone, and you never turned your back on a guy holding a pool cue."

"How many years did you do that, Doug?"

"I was in uniform for eleven years. I spent another seven as a detective."

"That's not something I'd volunteer for."

"Didn't all of the law enforcement rangers get called in when they had the riots in Minneapolis?"

"That was a couple of years before my time."

Jill pushed the tray with the last few slices of pizza toward Everett. "I'm done, and

Doug should be done. Finish off the last pieces before we go over to the fire station to meet Rachel."

After glancing at me to make sure I was on board, he wolfed down the pizza and washed it down with Pepsi. "Are you both diving today?"

Jill sighed. "I'd prefer not to. I just warmed up from the last dive."

"Let's see if Rachel found anyone else to join us," I suggested.

There was a pickup hooked up to the fire department's boat, and an SUV parked next to the fire hall entrance. Everett parked on the street so he wasn't blocking the firemen's parking lot in case of a call.

Rachel was inside, already wearing a wetsuit under a sweatshirt. She was talking to a middle-aged man dressed in khaki slacks and a North Face jacket. She introduced him as one of the city councilmen.

We shook hands and introduced ourselves. "I saw Rachel hooking up the boat and wondered if she'd had a rescue call," the councilman said.

"The guy we're looking for is past rescuing," I replied. "We're into recovery."

"That's what Rachel said." He nodded and said goodbye.

"Budget issues?" I asked.

"He was just checking in. The councilmen and cops keep an eye on the fire hall. He saw that I was here alone and stopped in to make sure everything was okay." Rachel pointed to two wetsuits she'd set out. "These are the ones you guys wore last time we went out. Did they fit okay?"

"Aside from letting the ice-cold water seep in?" Jill asked.

"That's kind of the nature of wetsuits," Rachel replied.

"If you don't need me in the water, I'll stay topside," Jill said.

"That's not a problem as long as one of you partners up with me on the dive."

I picked up the larger suit and walked toward the locker room. "I'll be ready in a second, partner."

Rachel, Jill, and Everett were looking at a topographic map of the lake when I returned. Rachel pointed to a shallower area adjacent to areas marked off from their previous searches. "Let's look here," she suggested. "If the ice pushed toward shore when it broke up, it might've spread bones somewhere in here."

Everett decided he'd check out the Blind Pig and the municipal liquor store while we dove.

We helped Rachel load diving gear into the boat. After changing into wetsuits and donning jackets, we drove to the lake and launched the fire department's watercraft.

Rachel yelled to be heard over the noise of the outboard as she steered us across the choppy water. "I'll anchor at the edge of the search area. Jill's going to stay in the boat while Doug and I swim a loop toward shore and back."

Rachel glanced at Jill's hip. "You're still armed, right?"

Patting her hip, Jill nodded. "Do you anticipate a problem?"

Rachel shook her head. "I never anticipate a problem. I like to be prepared if there is a problem. A woman sitting alone in a boat might attract undue attention."

"I'll be prepared."

Rachel watched the GPS coordinates until she'd found the location she wanted, then dropped the anchor and deployed the diving flag. Jill helped us put on our tanks and gear.

The water seemed marginally warmer than it had been on our previous dive. That perception may have been due to my lowered expectations versus the shock of the stabbing cold during our first dive. I followed Rachel's hand signals, and we swam parallel paths away from the boat. We'd been in the water for about ten minutes when she signaled to me, indicating her discovery of something on the bottom. I swam over, while she used her hands to clear the silt away from something. The murkiness was settling by the time I arrived, and a row of vertebrae was visible below us. We felt in the mucky bottom, trying to locate more bones past the ends of the row she'd uncovered. Sadly, there were only three bones in the immediate area. Rachel retrieved them and put two of them into her bag. Then held out the third one, pointing to a spot where a piece of bone was missing. She shrugged, then placed the bone into our collection bag. I heard the hum of an outboard motor as we resumed our search.

As the approaching motor got louder, Rachel motioned for me to circle back in the direction we'd come from. We'd been swimming toward our boat for a few minutes, hearing the increasing noise of the approaching outboard motor. The water was clear enough to see our anchor rope extending from the boat to the bottom ahead of us. The white hull of a second boat pulled alongside our boat, which made me anxious.

I pointed to the two boats and gestured for Rachel to swim faster. She nodded, and we kicked harder and doubled our speed. Even at that pace, we were several minutes away from the boats. As we got within a few yards of the vessels, the anchor of the second boat bounced along the bottom, then rose toward our boat in jerks, as if someone was pulling it up hand over hand.

I kicked as hard as I could and swam with my arms, angling upwards toward the platform on the back of our boat. Rachel grabbed my arm and redirected me toward the ladder on the side, keeping me away from the propellers.

Rachel had her hands on the ladder when one of the outboard motors started. I pushed her butt, hoping to propel her into the boat, then I grabbed the ladder with one hand as the visiting boat's propeller spun. Both boats lurched forward, and I struggled to pull myself up the ladder as the water pulled at my tank and wetsuit. I was halfway out of the water when a black object tumbled into me, nearly knocking me off the ladder. I kicked off the swim fins and planted my feet on the ladder's bottom rung. Using every bit of my strength, I pulled myself up a ladder rung, stepped up another rung, then flipped myself, belly first, onto the boat's gunwale.

Feeling the full weight of the tank and gear, I pulled myself over the gunwale as the boat lurched ahead, bouncing atop the waves. Jill was struggling with someone who was holding her by the hair with one hand while steering the boat with the other.

I lunged forward and grabbed the back of the guy's sweatshirt. He lost his balance, causing him to turn the steering wheel, throwing all three of us against the boat's side. Jill broke free of his grip and rolled away from him. I yanked on the man's sweatshirt and flopped backwards, pulling him on top of me and away from Jill.

That move partially dislodged my swim mask, temporarily blinding me. The weight of the tank and gear made it difficult to move or react to the man's flailing. He slammed his fist into my face, knocking the swim mask off and causing me to see stars. I pulled him close, hoping to stay inside his reach so he couldn't throw another haymaker. My weight and the weight of my gear kept us on the bottom of the boat in an insane wrestling match.

I have no idea how long we'd struggled when he smashed into me, headfirst. Having no perception of what was happening and no time to reason, I tried to roll, which was limited by the tank strapped to my back. At some point, I realized the man wasn't struggling.

Pushing him off of me, I struggled to release the tank. The motor stopped, and I felt someone grab my arm. I drew back my fist to throw a punch when Jill yelled, "IT'S ME! STOP!"

I relaxed, slipped, and fell backward onto the tank. My vision was blurred, and my head hurt like hell. Jill had moved away from me and focused on something on the other side of the boat. A second later, I heard and felt a series of metallic clunks, followed by the sound of gunfire.

Jill took cover behind the opposite gunwale and fired a series of shots that sent spent brass cartridges bouncing around the inside of the boat. A moment later, I heard a nearby outboard motor race.

The body next to me groaned, and I reached over and groped for the man's arm. Through increasingly blurred vision, I saw Jill pull out her handcuffs and felt her wrestle the man's arm away from me.

"What in hell is going on?" I asked, trying to wipe my eyes.

"Your head is bleeding, and Rachel's in the water a hundred yards behind us."

Suddenly aware that the impact I'd felt when climbing the ladder was my diving partner, I yelled, "I'm fine. Get Rachel."

The motor surged, and the boat turned as I tried to wipe the blood from my eyes. I didn't recognize the man's face, but I couldn't see it clearly.

"Who is that?" I asked.

"Forget him!" Jill yelled. "We've got to find Rachel."

I reached over the side of the boat and scooped several handfuls of water onto my face, trying to clear the blood from my eyes. Jill scanned the water ahead of us, so I looked off to the sides. At some point, I saw the radio mic attached to the dashboard.

"Mayday. Mayday. Mayday. This is the National Park Service. We're in a boat on Rainy Lake, Black Bay. We have a woman overboard and another injured person onboard."

I dropped the mic and washed my face again, resuming my search for Rachel.

"THERE!" Jill yelled, pointing slightly to our left. I saw something yellow bobbing in the water.

"It's Rachel's floatation vest!"

Thoughts raced through my head as we approached the bobbing yellow vest. *Dear God, let Rachel still be alive.*

Jill slowed, then cut the motor as we approached the yellow vest. When we were a few feet away, an arm rose and waved to us.

A voice responded to my radio call, "Park Service, this is the Coast Guard. What's your situation?"

"We've located our woman overboard. I have a suspect under arrest with unknown injuries. There's a boat with a white hull moving northwest from us at high speed. It probably has damage from gunfire."

"How many people are in the other boat?" I asked Jill.

"One man. Black hair and beard."

I repeated that description to the Coast Guard, then I went to the back of the boat to help Jill retrieve Rachel.

Rachel was missing her mask, and her inflated yellow vest made helping her difficult. With great effort, we got her onto the swimming platform, then into the boat. She struggled out of her tank and vest. As she collapsed onto the deck, she asked, "What in hell just happened?"

"Do you recognize the guy on the deck?" I asked.

She blinked her eyes as if they were blurry, then focused. "Never seen him before. Who is he?"

I turned to Jill, who had collapsed alongside Rachel. "Are you okay?"

"Yeah, I'm fine."

I scooped another handful of water and threw it on my face, hoping to clear my vision. "They shot at us."

Jill leaned her head back. "Yeah. I think they hit the boat a couple of times. The waves made it difficult to aim. Even if I didn't hit him, I think my shots convinced the guy he didn't want to hang around to see what happened to his buddy."

"Yeah, your shots got his attention. He couldn't aim any better than you could in this choppy water, but even a gangbanger gets lucky and hits something once in a while."

The handcuffed man groaned, then his eyes blinked open. "What the hell?" He looked at me. "The bag is ours. If you..."

He looked from me to Rachel, then twisted to see Jill. "You guys are dead. Untie me."

"What's in the bag?" I asked.

"You're trying to steal it, and you don't even know what's in it?"

The radio came to life. "Park Service, this is The Border Patrol. We're approaching Black Bay from the northwest. Can you see us?"

The guy stared at me and frowned. "What the hell? You're park rangers?"

Ignoring him, I wiped my eyes again and looked at the compass. Toward the northwest, I saw a dark object approaching. "I see something." I waved.

"Do you still require assistance?"

"Ten-four. We have an injured diver and a handcuffed suspect."

Five minutes later, a boat with two Border Patrol officers pulled alongside us. They threw bumpers over the side and tied up. The male officer inspected my forehead and applied gauze as his female partner knelt next to Rachel, whom she apparently knew.

"What happened to you?" the man asked.

"Our suspect head-butted me."

"Like hell I did," the handcuffed man said. "We were...helping these guys when someone hit me in the back of the head."

Jill reached down and picked up a small fire extinguisher from the deck. "I guess these are good for more than fires."

"What happened to the white boat?" I asked the BP agent.

"It crossed into Canada. We notified the RCMP and OPP, but they didn't have anyone in the area."

"Our *suspect* asked if we'd recovered a bag."

The female Border Patrol agent turned toward her partner and shook her head slightly. Then, she looked at me. "We know Rachel. Who are you two?"

I introduced us, and Jill showed them her credentials. "We're searching for additional remains of the body tied to the anchor."

"Did you notice a black buoy when you crossed from town?"

I shook my head, and Rachel said, "No."

"Do you require additional assistance returning to town?" the female agent asked Rachel.

"I think we're capable of getting ourselves back. We'll stow our gear and motor back." She glanced at the handcuffed man. "What about him?"

"He assaulted two federal agents," Jill replied.

"Would you like us to transport your suspect back to town so you can deal with your first aid issues?"

"Yes, thank you," I replied.

They motored away with the guy, and we helped Rachel stow the diving gear. I asked Jill, "What happened?"

"I was sitting in the boat and heard them approaching. They waved, like they were friendly, then pulled alongside. The guy with the beard asked if I'd seen their fishing buoy. He said they'd marked a hot spot, then lost track of it."

"And you didn't tell them to leave, or you'd shoot them?" I asked.

"They didn't display any firearms, nor did they act threateningly. I asked where they thought the buoy was, and the guy pointed in the direction where you two were diving. Then, he said, "There it is!""

I grimaced. "And when you looked, they jumped into the boat and disarmed you."

"I did NOT look and let them disarm me. One of them rocked the boat, I lost my footing, then he jumped in and tackled me as I was drawing my weapon."

Rachel strapped the last tank into place, then looked at Jill. "They didn't know you were a cop."

Jill looked down at the oversized Minnesota Vikings sweatshirt she was wearing. "I found this stowed in a locker when I got cold. I never identified myself as an officer. Everything went down too fast after that."

"You didn't notice that they didn't have any fishing gear?" I asked.

"They might've had a fishing rod propped up in a corner. I don't remember."

"They couldn't locate something they were supposed to retrieve," Rachel surmised as she started the outboard motor. "Like I said, it's not a safe place to be a woman alone in a boat."

# Chapter 11

We followed the Border Patrol boat back to the I-Falls boat launch, where they turned into what was apparently their marina slip. Rachel took us to the dock alongside the public launch, where two fishermen were in line to launch their boats behind two men who struggled to get their boat centered on their trailer, while the waves pushed it to the side every time they thought it was ready.

Jill watched them as Rachel and I tied the dive boat to the dock's cleats. Seeing Jill's interest in the bumbling operation, Rachel joked, "You should come here on the fishing opener. There is a line of boats and trailers a block long waiting to launch, and people discovering every mode of boat launch failure."

"Boat launch failure?"

"People get rushed and lose their minds. I've seen people launch boats without installing the drain plug, so they start sinking as soon as their boat is off the trailer. Others forget to release the straps holding the boat down, and there are always the rookies who don't know how to back a trailer down the ramp. I've seen guys try eight or ten times before someone behind them offers to back up for them."

"I'll talk to the guys waiting in line," I suggested, pulling my badge and credentials out of a dry bag in the boat. "I assume they'll let an injured cop in ahead of them."

Rachel waved over her shoulder as she walked to the parking lot to retrieve the trailer. "Good luck with that!"

I walked up to the two waiting boaters and explained that we had an injured person on board and wanted to get ahead of them in line. Both of them looked at the bloody gauze taped to my forehead, then pulled their rigs ahead, making an opening for Rachel. While I did that, I saw the two Border Patrol officers lead our suspect to a waiting SUV. They joined me on the dock as Rachel backed the boat trailer down the ramp.

One of them stepped into our boat as I released it from the cleats. "I'll put it on the trailer, if you don't mind."

I threw the second line into the boat and gestured for him to take over. I turned to the female agent and said, "I'm happy to let someone else take over that task. I'm not even a rookie, and it wouldn't have gone well in this wind."

Chuckling, the agent nodded. "The only good thing about the wind is it keeps the mosquitoes away."

"I bet half of them have blown into the next county."

The boat slid onto the trailer, and the agent clipped the trailer line to the front, then signaled Rachel to pull it out. Jill sat on a locker built into the side, alternately holding her side and shivering.

The female agent put her hands on my shoulders and turned me to inspect the bandage on my forehead. "You're leaking. We should take you to the ER."

"The guy headbutted me, so there's not really a cut or anything that can be stitched."

"I think the doctors might want to run a concussion protocol." She looked at Jill as Rachel pulled the boat and trailer ahead. "I don't know what's going on with your partner, but she doesn't look comfortable. She should probably be seen, too."

We talked as we made our way to where Rachel was strapping the boat to the trailer and picking off bits of seaweed. "Where are you taking our prisoner?"

"We've got a holding cell in our office."

"They asked Jill if she'd seen a black buoy."

"That's really odd. Fishermen use day-glow orange or yellow markers, and they're hard to see in heavy waves. A black buoy would be invisible in this chop. I suppose they had GPS coordinates that would put them right on top of the spot the buoy had been dropped."

We stopped at the trailer, where the male agent was helping Jill climb down from the boat. She grimaced every time she took a step. I checked on Jill while the female agent spoke to Rachel.

"You're in pain."

"Now that the adrenaline is wearing off, I feel the bruises from being tackled in the boat."

"The Border Patrol agent suggested that you and I go to the ER for a checkup."

"I think I'm just bruised."

"Let's let a doctor decide, okay?"

"I'll probably feel worse tomorrow, so we should at least pick up some Ibuprofen."

* * *

I was sitting in an exam room with the wetsuit peeled down to my waist. There was a knock on the wall, and Rachel asked, "Are you decent?" and then pulled back the curtain without waiting for an answer.

"Most people wait for a reply before barging into an exam room."

She handed me a paper shopping bag. "I brought your clothes."

"All the more reason to ask before entering. You knew I didn't have clothes."

"I can't believe a cop with as much experience as you have is bashful."

I pulled a t-shirt out of the bag and pulled it over my head. "What have you heard from the Border Patrol?"

Rachel snorted and turned her back as I pulled pants out of the bag. "You know how it is. They can't comment about an ongoing investigation."

"So, they didn't happen to be in the area."

"I see them out patrolling the lake all of the time. It may have been a coincidence that they were the closest boat."

After peeling off the wetsuit and pulling on my pants, I said, "I don't believe in coincidences." I put the wetsuit into the bag and added, "You can turn around. I'm decent."

She accepted the bag and nodded. "I checked on Jill first. She's waiting for the radiologist to read her X-rays." Rachel inspected the Steri-strips on my forehead. "That'll hardly leave a scar. How is your headache?"

"It's nothing a few Tylenols won't handle."

Rachel gave me a look. "Tough guy, huh?"

"Over the years, I've been banged up quite a few times. This is no worse than what I experienced playing high school football."

A man's head peeked around the curtain and asked, "Investigator Fletcher?"

"Come on in."

The visitor wore a Border Patrol stenciled vest. Aside from the captain's bars on his shoulders and his graying hair, he looked like the agents who'd rescued us. He nodded to Rachel, who smiled in acknowledgement. "I'm Captain Mason. How are you doing?"

"I've got a headache and a patched forehead. Other than that, I'm fine."

"Rachel, could I have a minute with Investigator Fletcher?"

"Sure, Glenn. I was leaving."

"Don't go too far. We'd like to get your statement about the boat event."

"At your offices?"

"Please, if that's convenient."

Rachel walked out of the room, and the captain waited until he thought she wouldn't hear what was said. "It sounds like you guys were lucky."

I nodded. "I'm glad your people were nearby. Were you able to locate the boat that showed up with the bad guys?"

A hint of a smile formed on Mason's lips. "Let's say, we know where it is and leave it at that."

"The other suspect shot at us. That's a high-level federal felony."

"We need to have this discussion in a more secure location. I'll have an officer drive you there once you're released."

"We have a ride."

"Everett is already in our break room. He can drive you back to your accommodations when we're through."

I lowered my voice. "I hope we didn't mess up a sting."

Mason shook his head. "Not here. I'll see you at our office."

"Have you spoken to my partner, Jill?"

"Yes. We'll get the rest of her statement after you're discharged."

I stopped Mason as he took a step toward the curtain. "Will we be able to interview the guy who assaulted us?"

"Uh, no. He's on his way to Duluth."

"But..."

"We'll discuss that at our office."

* * *

A young Border Patrol officer was doing something on her phone in the waiting area. She looked up when we walked out of the exam room, then put her phone away. "Doug and Jill Fletcher?"

"That's us."

"I'm here to transport you to the CBP building." She stared at Jill's arm, which was in a sling. "Are you in a lot of pain? Do we need to stop at a pharmacy or something?"

"I'm fine."

The trip from the small hospital to the brick CBP office took less than five minutes. Our driver was silent until she turned off Highway 11. "The Voyageurs National Park Headquarters is just one block down the road."

Our escort led us through a door that she unlocked with a key card. Once inside the office area, we placed our firearms in lockers and walked through a metal detector. As promised, Everett was sitting in a conference room reading something on his cell phone.

"Hey, guys! I was beginning to think you were close to death."

"You know how ERs go. We weren't dying, so we weren't their top triage priority."

As we spoke, Captain Mason walked into the room with the two agents who'd rescued us. I walked over and shook their hands. "Thanks for the backup."

They nodded and smiled, then we all sat around the table. Captain Mason took out a small recorder and set it in the center of the table. After introducing himself and his agents, he had us repeat our names and job titles.

"Aren't you going to include Rachel?" I asked.

Mason shook his head. "She's been interviewed separately. She doesn't have a need to know what I'm about to discuss with you."

"Fair enough," I replied.

"Tell us what the guys said about a buoy."

I gestured to Jill. "When the boat first came alongside me, they asked if I'd seen their black fishing buoy. They said something about having marked a hot fishing spot."

"You're sure they said a black buoy?"

"Yes, a black buoy."

Mason walked to a map of Rainy Lake mounted on the wall and pointed to an area on the park border. "And you were about here, in Black Bay, correct?"

"I'm not sure exactly where we were, map wise," Jill replied. "Rachel used a GPS to get us back to the site where the anchor and bones had been found."

Mason nodded. "This is the location she'd pointed out. Your recollection is no different from hers?"

"She did all of the navigation," Jill replied. "We were passengers."

Mason nodded, then took his seat. "My agents have been working with the RCMP and Ontario Provincial Police. Drugs from the US are being dropped in the lake. Canadian smugglers are retrieving them."

"That's why you were close to us," I stated.

Mason shook his head. "We were watching a spot about four miles from your location. Your story about the boaters asking about a black buoy contradicts what our informant told us."

"Your informant is lying or has been compromised," I said.

Mason steepled his hands and closed his eyes. "We need you to temporarily suspend your skeleton recovery operation." He looked at Jill and said, "You were either very lucky or very good this afternoon, Investigator Fletcher. The two men on the boat who approached you work for a cartel that's known for eliminating witnesses and people who stumble onto their operations."

"I should've been more suspicious. However, they were on the boat before I realized it."

"Did you learn anything from the man we arrested?" I asked.

"He's a pawn. In many respects, it would've been better for our operation if he'd escaped. On the other hand, you stumbling onto them as something other than Border Patrol agents, may protect our larger operation."

Jill nodded. "I was wearing a Minnesota Vikings sweatshirt. My badge and weapon weren't visible, and I never identified myself as a law enforcement officer."

"Are they using drones to make the drops?" I asked.

"We think so, although the bags of drugs they are dropping are larger than most civilian drones could deliver."

"As you said, a black buoy is hard to locate. Is there a radio beacon enclosed in the shipment?"

Mason looked at his female agent. "What do you think?"

"We're scanning radio frequencies and getting nothing. I think they're doing something lower tech, like using paint that shows up when hit by an infrared light. They probably search for it after dark with night-vision goggles."

"Why were they boating around us in the middle of the afternoon?" Jill asked.

"We think they had the area around the drop under surveillance in case a fisherman snagged the buoy. You were too close and were lingering too long. They got nervous."

I placed my hands on the table, preparing to stand. "So, we're through recovering bones, at least until your operation is done. I guess we'll focus on finding someone who recalls what happened in 1989."

"There is one thing you could do for us."

"Besides not bothering Mr. Bauer and his lazy dog?" I asked.

Mason glanced at his agents, who seemed to be suppressing smiles. "We'd like Mr. Bauer to remain off the radar. Your visit to his cabin was...unwelcome."

I nodded my understanding.

"Someone has been tipping off the cartel about our operations. We'd like you to plant some misinformation."

I leaned back in the chair and crossed my arms. "That's risky for the person planting the information and can blow up in your face. If you're thinking about us being the source, it has to be done in a credible way. We've been careful about only passing 'need to know' information to other law enforcement people. Us leaking confidential information to someone without their need to know it would raise flags."

Mason nodded. "We're counting on that. We'd like to do exactly that, tell people you're unable to talk about recent sensitive developments in your case. That way, people will think you've discovered something."

"How does that help?" I asked.

"You'll be lending credibility to the loose-lipped firemen, who are going to let slip that you and Rachel saw a duffel bag in the water before your confrontation with the other boat."

Smiling, I replied, "Using loose-lipped firemen as the source of misinformation?"

"Rachel is the chief, and she's reliably silent about what she sees and knows. On the other hand, Lance circulates around the cafés and bars and is notoriously chatty. He'll have heard about the bag from Rachel. Your 'no comment' will lend credibility to Lance's inside information."

"Is there anyone special we should 'no comment' to?" Jill asked.

Mason nodded his head. "You met Vic English at the fire station, right?"

"We've actually met Vic a couple of times. Do you think he's the person leaking information about your operations?"

"We don't think it's Vic, directly. We think it's Vic's *big mouth* bragging about his inside information to anyone who'll listen."

I looked at Everett. "We need to stop at Vic's favorite café on our way back to Davidson's. I feel a little chilled, and a cup of coffee might warm me up."

We stood and shook hands with the Border Patrol agents. The female agent leaned close to Jill and whispered something. As we walked to the Park Service pickup, I asked, "What did she tell you?"

"The Canadians had the white boat under aerial surveillance. They recorded a video of the guy tying up the boat. He was only using one hand because he'd apparently suffered a gunshot wound in the other arm or shoulder." Jill paused, smiling. "I hit him, *and* there were several bullet holes in the boat's hull, too."

Everett smiled and glanced at me. "You're married to Annie Oakley!"

* * *

The Family Café was nearly empty when we walked in. We sat at a table near the kitchen and ordered coffee. Young Everett ordered a cinnamon roll. The waitress had just topped off our coffee when Vic walked in with two of his cronies.

Seeing us, he let his friends take a table near the door, then he walked over to our table and pulled out a chair. "You guys had quite a day, and it looks like you might've lost the fight. I heard Jill even took a couple of potshots at a guy."

Everett smiled. "She hit him from a moving boat."

185

I frowned at Everett, who shut up and looked contrite. "Vic, you know we can't comment on an operation."

"Oh, fer Christ's sake, I'm a cop."

"You're a retired cop, and you don't need to know."

Vic rolled his eyes and stood. "Have a nice day."

Jill smiled and leaned close and whispered, "I think he was being facetious when he told us to have a nice day."

I nodded and smiled at Everett. "Good job. You hooked him with your comment about Jill's shooting. And your guilty expression was perfect."

"I thought you were really mad at me," he whispered.

"Finish your roll and drive us back to Davidson's. I'm hungry."

Jill stood and nodded. "Some of us saved our appetites for supper instead of eating a roll at four o'clock in the afternoon."

Everett wiped his mouth with a paper napkin. "Don't worry, I'll be ready to eat again by six. I think Laney and I are having pizza again."

# Chapter 12

The lodge's restaurant/bar was full when we walked over from our cabin. I talked to Megan. After I explained that we weren't badly injured, she promised to come and find us by the fireplace when a table opened up. Jill was staring into the crackling and popping pine logs that were spitting embers at the fireplace's protective screen.

"You look like someone ran over your dog," I said as I sat next to her.

"Even though we know it is Flacowski's body, we can't find a motive for murdering him."

"I think Peggy Mischke probably hit the nail on the head when she said one of their former neighbors had packed up his daughter and vacated their house unexpectedly."

"So, what do we do next? Are we going to dig through old property records at the courthouse and find all of the owners from the '80s?"

I picked up a wrought iron poker and adjusted a log that was starting to slip off the grate. "There must be someone who remembers the name of that family."

"What if they left because of something else? We could spend weeks tracking down the property records and owners. Hell, half of them are probably dead." Jill's eyes looked tired, and her body seemed to sag. "What if it wasn't them, but some other family who lived farther away from Mischke's? We'll never find them."

"Let's talk to my confidential informant. I saw him sitting at the end of the bar."

Grimacing, Jill shook her head. "You talk to Booger. I don't have another pair of jeans to change into if he sneezes on me again."

"Come on. You're worrying the girl working at the check-in desk who's been watching us."

We threaded our way past the tables filled with fishermen. Most were laughing, probably repeating lies about catches from years past. At least, that had been my experience with fish stories. My patched forehead and Jill's sling caught everyone's attention.

I wedged myself between Booger and a guy who looked like he'd just walked out of the Orvis store at the mall. He was dressed in brand new clothes with stray threads at the corners of his shirt pockets and belt loops. After apologizing to the stylish angler for bumping his elbow, I turned to Booger. "How's your beer?"

Ignoring my question, Booger asked, "What happened to your head?"

"I bumped into a door in the dark." I signaled the bartender for a refill and turned back to Booger.

Jill slipped alongside him, with her back against the wall. Booger turned toward Jill and leaned back, as if she was too close for him to focus on. "What happened to your shoulder? Did you bump into a door, too?"

Ignoring the question, Jill said, "Hi, Booger. Are you doing okay?"

The bartender placed a fresh frosty mug in front of Booger, and I handed him the nearly empty mug.

"Hey! I wasn't done with that one!" he protested.

"Drink this cold one instead," I suggested.

Booger mumbled something about wasting beer, then he took a swallow from the fresh mug. "What are you two up to tonight? Did you run out of people to spy on, or are you too injured to work?"

"I've got a problem you might be able to solve."

Booger wrinkled his nose and turned to Jill. "What's your partner been smoking? He seems to think I might know something he doesn't."

I saw Jill bracing herself. In addition to the beer, Booger's breath smelled a bit like he'd been chewing raw garlic. "My partner doesn't know a lot of things, and folks say you're an observant guy."

Booger snorted, which sprayed a bit of snot on the bar and into his beer. He didn't seem to notice. "What do you think I might've observed?"

"We know that the guy with the anchor tied around his ankle was working for Mischke right before he disappeared. His name was Will Flacowski. We think he might've thought he was quite a lady's man, and we heard a rumor that he might've gotten some woman pregnant."

"What's it to you?"

"We're thinking that maybe the woman's husband or father got into it with Flacowski and killed him."

"I don't know anyone named Flacowski."

"This happened back in the '80s."

The '80s? Hell, I can't remember what I did this morning."

"We think this Flacowski guy was a real hotshot. He'd been thrown out of the Army."

"A veteran?" Booger asked.

"He'd been in Vietnam. He re-enlisted after the war and went to parachute school."

Booger frowned. "What in hell is parachute school? Are you saying he was airborne?"

"Yeah, that's it. He even wore a ring with a parachute and a skull."

"I don't know nothin' about an airborne guy named Flacowski."

"Are you sure? He called himself Will Flaco."

Booger swirled his beer and took a drink. "There was an airborne guy who hung around here years ago named Will. A real a-one asshole. Cocky shit who rode a motorcycle. Is that who you're talking about?"

Jill gave me a look like she wanted me to jump in. I shook my head. When you've got someone talking, you don't break their train of thought. She nodded to Booger. "That might be him. What can you tell me about him?"

"I already told you what I knew. He had a chip on his shoulder. Always talking about shit that he'd done in 'Nam. I knew he was bullshitting because nobody who was really there talked about what happened when they were around ordinary folks."

"He rode a motorcycle? We heard he lived in a trailer at Mischke's place."

"He lived in the trailer, but he rode around on his motorcycle."

"I guess he must've thought he was quite the lady's man."

Booger snorted again, blowing a fine mist that mostly landed on his shirt. "He wasn't no lady's man. They saw right through his line of bullshit. At least the adult women did. I think some of the younger girls thought he was hot stuff. I imagine they all figured that out for themselves."

"He hung out with the younger women and teenage girls?"

"I think he was buying booze for them that were too young. He was kind of a parasite. Putting on big airs and trying to get the women drunk so he could...you know."

"Was there any special woman or girl who got hurt by him?"

Booger stared at Jill's sling. "Have you ever been hurt by a guy?"

"I suppose every woman has stories about the jerks who broke their heart."

"No, I mean, have you been *hurt*?"

"I had a boyfriend who got a little rough once. I showed him the door."

Booger raised his beer. "Good for you!" He looked at Jill's empty hands, then looked up and down the bar. "Hey, where's your beer?"

"I'm not much of a beer drinker."

"Not a beer drinker? What are you doing in a bar?" Booger waved to catch the bartender's attention. "Hey, Mick! Get this lady one of whatever she wants. Put it on my tab."

The bartender walked down to Jill, trying to keep from smiling. "Booger's buying. What would you like?"

"A white wine?"

The bartender turned away and pulled a bottle of wine out of the refrigerator. He set the glass in front of Jill, then he winked at Booger. "You sly old dog."

Booger flipped his hand dismissively. "It ain't like that. This one's a lady."

Jill smirked as she sipped her wine. "I don't like calling you Booger. What's your name?"

After looking at Jill for a moment as if testing her sincerity, he replied, "Lyle. Lyle Sertich."

Finally hearing his name, Jill recalled Randy Mischke's suggestion to use Lyle as a local resource. "Thanks for the wine, Lyle."

"You're entirely welcome. I haven't had a real conversation with a woman in years."

"You were telling me about Will, the...airborne guy. He hurt some woman?"

"No one knows for sure, but something happened when he took her on that motorcycle of his. They were gone a long time, and when they came back, she wasn't the same. Clothes dirty, tears streaming down her face, and her pushing him away like he'd done something bad to her."

Jill glanced at me, then turned her attention back to Sertich. "This was right about the time Will disappeared?"

Booger shrugged. "I don't know exactly when that happened, or when he stopped coming around. But it was all about the same time."

"Was this girl's family staying in a cabin, or was she one of the local residents?"

He froze with the beer halfway to his mouth. "You don't know?"

"No."

"That was Mischkes' daughter."

Hiding her surprise, Jill asked, "How old was she when this happened?"

"I don't know. She wasn't old enough to drink in a bar. I suppose she was just a teenager."

Jill's eyes locked with mine, and her breathing got ragged. She composed herself and asked, "Will took Mischkes' daughter on a motorcycle ride, and something bad happened that messed up her clothes and made her cry?"

"We all saw them ride back."

"Was it local common knowledge?"

"I guess so. I mean, there were a bunch of us cleaning fish when Will brought her back. She rode off on her bicycle. Max ran after her, but she wasn't having anything to do with him after that."

"Max Davidson ran after her?"

"Yeah. I think Max had a crush on her. She wasn't too interested in him. I think she kind of liked bad boys, like Will."

"Who else was with you when you saw that?"

"Max, Karl, and I had been guiding folks. We were cleaning fish for three or four guys from the Cities."

"Karl Peterson was there, too?"

"Yeah. As a matter of fact, Karl got into Will's face over it. Karl knocked him down, and Will was ready to fight." Lyle chuckled at the memory. "I think Karl dared Will to take a punch. Will sized him up, then made some comment and rode off."

Megan tapped my shoulder. "I've got a table for you."

I nodded and dug a twenty dollar bill out of my pocket and handed it to her. "Hang onto it for a few minutes. Okay?"

"Did you see the Mischke girl after that?" Jill asked.

"Oh sure. She was around town and such. I don't recall her ever coming back around here after that. I suppose maybe her mother kept her on a short leash."

"Does she still live in the area?"

"I haven't seen her in years. Hell, I doubt I'd recognize her after all these years."

"Are you doing okay with your beer?" I asked, sensing that Jill had run out of questions.

Booger looked at the mug, then nodded. "I could probably drink another after a bit, if you're buying."

I signaled the bartender to bring another beer. "A table just opened up. Would you like to join us for supper?"

Booger lifted his beer. "I've got my supper. Thanks."

Jill hesitated, then put her hand on the old man's shoulder. "Doug, our confidential informant is Lyle. Randy and Peggy said he'll be a great resource."

I looked at the grizzled old man, trying to picture him as a credible witness. I decided to test his memory. "We heard you played on the Bronco's state tournament hockey teams."

The old man's eyes got misty, and he nodded. "Them were the days. Two championship teams. I had a tryout with the Chicago Blackhawks scout."

"Wow! What an honor."

"I thought I was hot shit, you know, the star. That Blackhawks scout could skate faster backwards than I could going forward. He said they wanted me to come to Chicago for a tryout. My girlfriend didn't want to move all the way to Chicago." Lyle shook his head. "I was a stupid kid. Instead, I got drafted by the Army, married her after boot camp, and spent a year in 'Nam." He chuckled. "I came home from 'Nam and she was living with one of my buddies in California. She didn't even take the time to write a Dear John letter."

"Life takes strange turns," I replied. "Are you sure you don't want to join us for supper?"

Megan interrupted us and pointed to a group of three men who'd been sitting at a high-top table and were now looking at a framed photo. "Excuse me, those guys would like to talk to you," she said, nodding to Lyle.

He smiled and carried his beer to the group who seemed captivated by whatever Lyle was telling them.

"What's up with those guys?" I asked Megan as she led us to our table.

"They saw the picture of the championship hockey team and newspaper article about Booger being named to the All-

State hockey team. They were excited when I said he was sitting at the bar."

"Does that happen often?" Jill asked.

"Once in a while," Megan said. "People think it's pretty cool to meet the guys in the pictures."

"The guys? More of those hockey players hang around here?"

"Booger is the only hockey player who's still around. A couple of the old-time fishing guides stop in once in a while. The fishermen love hearing their stories." After seating us, she pointed to a giant walleye mounted on the wall. "Karl Peterson caught that. He claims it's the unofficial state record. I overheard him tell some guys he never had it weighed on a certified scale, so it can't be called the state record."

"How much did it weigh?" I asked.

"Dead fish aren't my thing. There's a little plaque under it. I think it has Karl's name, the date, and the weight."

I walked to the mount, which had a light patina of dust. The fish was close to a yard long and the brass plaque under it read *Karl Peterson, May 22, 1968, 18 pounds.* Below the mounted fish was a framed newspaper article about the official state record fish being moved to the Chik-Wauk Museum. It weighed 17 pounds 8 ounces and looked about the same size as Karl's mounted walleye.

Walking back to the table, I thought about the fishing scale my dad kept in his tackle box to weigh our catch. I recalled the scale showing a different weight, usually plus or minus ten percent, each time we tugged on it. Chuckling to myself, I thought, *I bet that's how you weighed your record, Karl Peterson. Better to have a good story than risk a certified scale showing a pound or two less than your hand-held scale.*

When I returned to my seat, Jill asked, "What's funny about the dead fish?"

"It brought back a memory of fishing with my dad."

"You never talk about your dad."

"I guess those memories are buried deep. He pops to mind every once in a while, when I see or smell something familiar. I think of him every time I use WD-40. He used it to lubricate everything from door hinges to his shotgun."

She leaned across the table and whispered, "Did you hear the story Lyle told me?"

"I heard some of it. Flacowski gave Mischkes' daughter a motorcycle ride, and she was messed up afterward."

"Not messed up, Doug. She was rattled, and her clothes were disheveled and dirty. I think Flacowski raped her."

"We need to find someone to corroborate Lyle's story."

"Max Davidson and Karl Peterson were there. Let's ask them."

Jill started to stand, and I put my hand on her arm. "Not tonight."

"Why not?"

"We need to do this in the daylight, and when you haven't had wine."

"I'm fine."

"You are *not* fine. You're keyed up with adrenaline pulsing through your veins. We're going to discuss this with Everett in the morning, and then we'll interview Max Davidson."

"What about the Mischkes? When are we going to confront them?"

"If we get a similar story from Max Davidson or Karl Peterson, we'll talk to the sheriff and the county attorney. They'll probably want to execute a search warrant and then take both of the Mischkes in for questioning."

"I want to be there."

"What's our job?"

"What do you mean? We're investigators. We investigate."

"And we let the local authorities make the arrests and prosecute the criminals. We'll watch the interviews from the other room. If they've got the situation under control, we'll step back and let them carry the ball."

Jill drew a deep breath and let it out slowly, like she was counting to ten.

"You want to shoot someone. That's not going to happen."

"You know damned well I wouldn't shoot anyone unless they were pointing a gun at one of us."

I smiled. "I'm glad we're clear on that."

Misreading Jill's anger, Megan rushed over and apologized for not taking our orders sooner.

"It's okay. We're just having a quiet dinner conversation. I'll have the special."

Megan froze. "There is no special tonight."

"Fine, I want a sirloin steak, medium rare, with a salad and baked potato."

Jill studied her wine glass for a moment and lifted her sling. "What do you suggest for someone eating with one hand?"

"Um, probably the walleye sandwich."

"I'll have a walleye sandwich with slaw and fries." When Megan left, Jill asked, "What do you expect to find with a search warrant after all these years?"

"A motorcycle."

* * *

We ate a leisurely dinner, listening to another group of fishermen who'd joined Lyle as he recounted hockey stories. Megan rushed back and forth with orders and checked to see if we needed refills, then offered us take-out containers for our leftovers.

By the time we'd finished supper, Lyle had returned to his customary seat at the end of the bar. Outside of the lodge, Jill looped her arm in mine and steered me toward the lake. "Look at it, Doug. It's like someone threw orange, red, and yellow paint across the sky and lake." She stepped in front of me and pulled my arms around her waist. "The sunset is such a contradiction to our grisly investigation. This beautiful moment of solitude is surreal when I think about how a man's life ended when he was dropped into the lake with an anchor tied to his foot."

We watched the colors change from the palette of red and orange to deep purple. The first stars started twinkling when I noticed the forest was starting to hum. "We've got to go."

Jill sighed, continuing to stare toward the west. "I suppose so."

"I mean, now. I can hear the mosquitoes revving up."

We fast-walked back to our cabin, arriving with a cloud of mosquitoes that I batted away before opening the door. I swatted a few persistent pests who'd been in our clothes or hair while Jill went into the bathroom. By the time she came out, I'd killed nearly a dozen mosquitoes.

"What happened to the rest of the anchor rope?" she asked.

"The rest of what anchor rope?"

"There was only a foot of extra anchor rope with the foot. Mischke was a fisherman, so he must've had at least thirty or forty feet of rope on the anchor."

"I suppose the ice and weather frayed it and dragged the rest away."

"The knots were still intact."

"I don't know." I looked at Jill, who was still mulling the rope question. "This is going to keep you awake, isn't it?"

"I think my aching shoulder will be a bigger sleep problem."

* * *

My phone was charging on the nightstand, and the ringtones somehow fit with my dream, until Jill poked me and said, "Answer your phone."

"Fletcher," I said as I looked at the glowing alarm clock that showed 3:18.

"Look across the lake, toward Black Bay."

"Everett?"

"Yeah. Look outside."

Much of our lake view from the cabin was obscured by trees, so I couldn't see much of anything except the dock light over the boat launch area. I pulled on pants and a sweatshirt.

"Where are you going?" Jill asked.

"Everett says something is happening across the lake."

We dashed out of the cabin and walked to the dock where the boats were moored. Two figures stood at the end of the dock looking over the water. In the distance, I saw flashing blue and red lights, along with spotlights sweeping back and forth across the water. We joined Everett and Laney on the dock.

Everett glanced back when he heard our approaching footsteps. "I think the Border Patrol operation just ended."

"How long have you been watching?" I asked as I swatted the mosquitoes on my arms.

"I suppose like ten minutes. I was dropping Laney off when I saw the commotion." He paused as a spotlight stopped, apparently locking onto something floating in the water. "There was some gunfire initially. Now, it looks like they're trying to find someone, or something in the water. I think they're using a drone over the search area."

"How much gunfire?"

"I don't know. Maybe a dozen shots. I saw the flashes then heard the pop-pop-pop."

I patted his shoulder. "Are you sad you're not part of it?"

"Not if they're shooting at each other. I'm happy to be the ranger who never drew his weapon."

Laney turned to Jill and me, her face looking pale under the lights. "Are those your injuries from the fight in the boat?"

I gave Everett the evil eye. "The boat trip was a little rough."

Laney looked toward the flashing lights on the lake, then asked, "Have you ever been in a gunfight like that?"

"Never on the water," I replied.

Laney nodded, ignoring what I'd left unsaid as she swatted at the bugs swarming around us. "The mosquitoes are eating us alive. We're going inside." Laney pulled Everett's arm. "Walk me to my cabin. I need to get *some* sleep before my shift."

# Chapter 13

The next morning, Laney delivered our coffee and asked, "Does your arm hurt a lot?"

"It aches, but I'm okay."

Nodding, Laney asked, "The usual for both of you?" She had pronounced bags under her bloodshot eyes, but she was working and tried to look cheerful.

"Sure," Jill replied.

Before Laney left to put in our order, I asked, "Is Max Davidson around this morning?"

"I haven't seen him. Do you want me to check his office?"

"Yes, please."

As Laney left the dining room, Jill asked, "You want to talk to Davidson before getting the search warrant?"

"I think a private conversation would be enlightening."

Laney was back a moment later. "He's just finishing up something. He'll pop over in a couple of minutes."

We were nearly through with breakfast when Davidson walked into the dining room/bar. He spotted us, signaled Laney he'd like a cup of coffee, then took a chair across from Jill.

"You two are early birds." He looked at Jill's sling but didn't comment.

"We're not on vacation, so we're up and working," I replied.

"What do Park Service investigators do so early in the morning?"

"We're hoping to find a couple of witnesses to a possible crime."

Davidson was confused by that. "How can I help?"

"Do you remember the Mischkes' daughter?"

Surprise registered on Davidson's face. "Um, sure. I hung around with Belinda Mischke. Phew, that was a long time ago."

Jill smiled and said, "Lyle Sertich thought you had a crush on her."

Davidson chuckled and avoided the question. "You two are good investigators. No one knows Booger's real name is Lyle."

"Do you remember a vet who hung around with you guys? Lyle said the vet gave Belinda a motorcycle ride that didn't end well."

The smile slid off Davidson's face as if it had melted. "I don't recall a motorcycle accident."

Jill leaned close and spoke softly, "There wasn't an accident. The vet took Belinda for a long ride. She ran off when they returned, as if something bad had happened."

"Okay..."

"You, Karl, and Lyle were cleaning fish after guiding a group on the lake."

"Lyle has had a lot of alcohol since those days. I'm not sure his memory is reliable anymore."

"So, that didn't happen?" I asked.

"I don't recall it as Lyle told it."

"Tell us what you remember," Jill said. When Max didn't immediately reply, she added, "Maybe we should get Karl Peterson over for a cup of coffee. I understand he was filleting walleyes, too."

Max glanced around, as if making sure no one was listening. "Yes, there was something. I don't know what happened, and Belinda never said anything about the ride to me."

"You spoke to Belinda after that?"

Laney swept over to the table and collected our empty plates. "Is there anything else I can bring for you?"

"Bring a pot of coffee and three mugs to my office, please."

"Um, sure."

Davidson stood and nodded toward the door. I threw $40 on the table and followed him. We studied Davidson's office decor while waiting for Laney and the coffee. The knotty pine walls were covered with taxidermy mounted fish and pictures of fishermen. Two framed family photos stood on a credenza under a window that overlooked the shimmering lake.

We'd just settled in our chairs when Laney arrived with a platter. After setting out the carafe and mugs, Davidson smiled and said, "Thanks, Laney. Please close the door when you leave."

Davidson poured coffee, then leaned back into his chair with the steaming mug in his hand. He stared at the lake where a group of fishermen were loading gear into their boat. "I miss the simpler days when my only responsibilities were guiding fishermen to places I knew they'd catch fish, telling resort stories, and filleting fish. At the end of the day, we'd sit around a campfire with whoever was at the resort. I'd go to bed and sleep like a baby." He sighed and looked at me. "Now, I sit here doing bookkeeping, trying to hire people who will actually show up for their second shift, and worry if I'll have the cash flow to pay my key people over the winter."

"I think we all like to remember those simpler times." After a pause, I asked, "What happened to Belinda on her motorcycle ride with someone named Flaco or Flacowski?"

"Flacowski! That was his name. I'd forgotten."

Jill grew impatient when Max didn't expand on the comment. "Please fill us in on what happened that summer."

Davidson drew a breath and stared into his mug. "I probably should've said something back then, but I was a kid. I thought the grownups would take care of everything."

"Everything being?"

"Are sins of omission crimes?"

Jill looked at me. "I guess that depends. A person who knows about a crime may be abetting the criminal by not reporting it."

"Do I need a lawyer?"

"I think the criminal in this case is deceased, so there won't be an arrest or trial."

Max nodded. "Flacowski was a piece of work."

"Go on."

"I was like fourteen and he must've been about thirty. He was good-looking, had stories about his Vietnam bravery, and rode a motorcycle. He thought he was God's gift to women."

Jill nodded. "We heard that he hit on all the women at the resort."

"Most of them saw through his lines of bullshit. Anyone with a brain knew he was lying about his achievements. He claimed expertise in everything from being Rambo to driving in an Indy 500 race. If someone said they'd caught a big walleye, Flacowski talked about the bigger one he'd released. If someone talked about skiing, he'd talk about nearly winning an Olympic skiing medal. Of course, no one knew who came in fourth, so it was difficult to dispute his lies."

"Tell us about Belinda."

Davidson got a dreamy look. "Living in a resort is strange. Every week, a new group of vacationers arrives. I was oblivious to the hell my parents were going through. All I did was take orders to change sheets in the cabins, set out fresh towels, mop out the boats, pick up litter, fillet fish, and ride with Dad when he took garbage to the dump. I felt like a slave."

"Belinda," Jill repeated.

Davidson nodded. "I was a teenager, and I had a crush on a different girl every week. I was probably thirteen when Dad pulled me aside after I'd made a fool of myself by being overly helpful to a family who had a cute daughter. I remember him saying, 'Don't you EVER get friendly with one of the customers' daughters. Or worse yet, one of their wives. We rely on return business and word-of-mouth advertising. I can't afford to lose a customer because you've done something stupid with a cute girl.'"

"Belinda wasn't a customer's daughter," Jill suggested.

"Exactly. After Dad's lecture, I tried very hard to be professional around our customers. If there was ever a hint of a spark, whether they flirted with me, or I flirted with them, I'd get the evil eye. I actually believed that Dad would beat me within an inch of my life if I even took a hike in the woods with one of the visitors' daughters." Davidson paused. "Belinda and I went to school together, so we'd grown up together since grade school.

She was cute, smart, and totally not into me. We were buddies."

We sat silently while Davidson reflected on the past.

When he looked up, it was as if he'd been elsewhere and was surprised to see us. "Then, Belinda grew up. Girls mature faster than boys. All of a sudden, she had a girlish figure, and I was still into pulling pigtails. At some point, my hormones started flowing, and I saw her in a different light. You know, she went from my playground buddy, or that girl I teased on the school bus, to a young woman. We were walking away from the bus on the last day of school, and Belinda held my hand. When she walked to her house, I shook like I was frostbitten. The next time I saw her was like a month later, when she rode her bike over to see me. I was busy doing chores, and she helped while we talked. At the end of the day, we kissed behind a cabin."

"Then Flacowski showed up?"

Davidson shook his head. "That was the next year. Belinda and I had been 'dating' for a year. Of course, neither of us drove a car, but everyone knew we were an item. The few days when I wasn't slaving away at the resort, I'd ride my bike over to see her. She'd ride over and help me with the Saturday changeover." Max shook his head. "Life was so simple. We kissed a couple of times, but that was as far as our 'relationship' ever progressed. Then, Flacowski showed up."

"He worked for Mischkes?"

"Yeah, he helped Mr. Mischke in the machine shop. They moved an old travel trailer into the yard because he didn't have the money to rent a place around here in the summer when the city folks were paying big bucks to rent even dumpy cabins."

"And he charmed Belinda?"

Max nodded. "Belinda stopped biking over, and she was distant when I biked over there. I could tell she had stars in her eyes when she looked at Flacowski. Mr. Mischke saw it too, and he laid down the law to Flacowski. I guess Belinda and Flacowski couldn't be alone together anywhere around their place. Then, she biked over one day. I thought, 'hey, she's back!' But she'd come over here for a motorcycle ride with Flacowski. You know, out of Daddy's sight," he said, taking a breath. "I was busy cleaning fish, so I just watched as she got onto the motorcycle behind Flacowski. She wrapped her arms around him. I remember the huge smile she flashed at me as they drove off."

"What happened when they came back?" Jill asked.

"Belinda looked like she'd seen hell. Her face was smeared with dirt, and her clothes were rumpled and dirty. I waved at her, and she looked away. When Flacowski parked, she jumped off and ran to her bike. She rode away like the devil was chasing her."

"Did she ever tell you what happened with Flacowski?"

Max shook his head. "Not in words."

"Go on."

"She wasn't the same person after that. She never smiled, and she treated me like a leper. We went back to school the next fall, and it was like we'd never met. She wouldn't talk to me."

"Did you and Belinda graduate together?"

Max shook his head. "Belinda was a year older and left halfway through my freshman year. Nobody knew where she had gone."

"Did you ask Mr. Mischke?"

"No. He was a grown-up and kind of scary and tough."

"There must've been rumors," Jill suggested.

"Oh, yes. There were hundreds of rumors. Everything from she'd run away from home to she'd gotten pregnant and was living with relatives in Iowa."

"But you never knew exactly what happened to her?"

Davidson shook his head.

"Flacowski disappeared too, didn't he?" I asked.

"I guess so. I didn't see much of him after that. I was busy at the resort, so it's not like I would've run into him."

"Did he keep showing up here to hit on the vacationing women?"

"That stopped at some point. I don't know exactly when. I got the impression that my dad had given him the bum's rush because he didn't need Flacowski causing a rift with our customers."

When Davidson seemed talked out, I asked, "Do you think Mischke killed him?"

"Are you asking if I *know* that Mischke killed him? I have to say no. If you're asking if I *think* Mischke killed him..."

"Did Flacowski disappear about the same time Mischke's boat was found adrift?"

"I really can't say. I remember the boat incident because Dad, Lyle, Karl, and I took boats out to search for it. Dad found the boat and towed it back to Mischke's dock. We all met over there and Mischke had a fit because his good anchor was missing." Davidson got a funny look on his face. "It's odd because Mischke never thanked us. He was spouting off about a missing anchor and my dad got pissed. He told Mischke to find his own damn boat the next time it floated away. Mischke kind of settled down after that and thanked Dad for towing the boat back."

"That was right after a storm, right? The boat blew away in a rainstorm with heavy winds."

"Yeah, it had stormed the night before. The boat blowing away never made any sense. I mean, we all knew boats, motors, fishing equipment, and gear. I knew how to secure a boat to the dock before I was in kindergarten. Like everyone else around here, Mischke had big cleats on his dock to tie down his boat. There's no way that boat would blow away without taking the dock with it."

"Did the rope break?" Jill asked.

Max stared at her as if she'd slapped him. "No."

"What's the matter?" I asked.

"There wasn't a rope in the boat. Dad cut one of our ropes so he could tie his boat to the dock. His rope must've been attached to the missing anchor."

I set my mug aside and leaned on the desk. "I'm going to share something extremely confidential. You have to keep it to yourself until you hear it on the news. I'd like your opinion on what it means. Okay?"

"Um, sure."

"We found Flacowski's body with Mischke's anchor tied to the ankle. What does that mean to you?"

Max stared at me with his mouth open. "My God. Mischke tied his anchor to Flacowski's ankle and pushed him overboard. He must've used the rest of the anchor rope to tie him up."

Jill glanced at me, making sure I'd heard his explanation of what might have happened to the rest of the rope.

"And?"

"And he motored back to his dock and let his boat drift away, so it appeared the boat had been stolen."

There was a knock on the door as Max digested what he'd just said. Everett opened the door and stepped in. "Laney said you guys were over here." He saw Davidson's look of astonishment, and then at me. "What's up?"

I motioned for him to step into the office and close the door. "Max, tell Everett what you just said."

Max looked up at Everett. "Mischke must've tied Flacowski's foot to his anchor and pushed him overboard. Then, he set his own boat adrift, so it appeared it had been stolen."

Everett frowned. "Why would he do that?"

Davidson's breath grew ragged. "Because Flacowski raped Belinda."

Everett looked at me. "Who's Belinda?"

"She's Randy Mischke's daughter."

Everett raised his eyebrows. "Means, motive, and opportunity. Wow. Absolutely textbook."

I stood and looked at Max. "Not a word to anyone. Understood?" He nodded, then I said to Everett, "We're going to see the sheriff and county attorney. We need a search warrant. I hope there's a motorcycle somewhere on Mischke's property."

Outside of the office, I turned to Jill. "Do you think you can locate Belinda Mischke?"

"I can search for driver's licenses, real estate transactions, criminal history, marriages, and social media."

"Can we leave you here to do that while we get a search warrant?"

"Sure. But I'd like to be along when you arrest that sonofabitch. Can you imagine tying up someone, then pushing him out of a boat with an anchor tied to his ankle? That's heartless."

"So is raping your employer's underage daughter." I nodded toward Max. "Keep an eye on him. Make sure he doesn't call Mischkes or leave."

Max shook his head. "We're all looking for justice. I'm not calling anyone or going anywhere."

# Chapter 14

Everett and I walked to the Park Service pickup, which had garnered the attention of two fishermen who were having a discussion alongside the driver's door. They stepped aside as we approached, and the older of the two wore a red cap advertising a fishing lure company. He nodded at us and then focused on Everett. "You're the ranger Laney can't stop talking about," he said.

Everett blushed and nodded to them without comment. As he stepped into the pickup, the other fisherman said, "You must be quite a catch. We saw her standing outside the lodge's kitchen door, saying a final goodbye to her old boyfriend."

"What's up with that?" I asked as we drove away.

"Laney and I talked last night, which is why we were standing by the lake at 3 AM. She's been putting up with a lot of crap from her long-time boyfriend. I told her she shouldn't compromise her principles just to hang onto a guy who is obviously using her."

"I suppose it was hard for her to admit she was in a bad situation."

"You evaded Laney's shooting question last night," Everett said, glancing at me. "Have you been shot at?"

"Once or twice."

"Did they miss?"

I laughed. "I'm here, and unscarred."

"Good."

"Jill's been hit a couple of times."

"You're joking."

"Her vest saved her life once."

"Jill? She seems…"

I pulled out my phone when we reached the road. "I need to warn the sheriff that we're coming. He may want one of his investigators to sit in with us. I hope he can find someone from the county attorney's office, too."

"Go ahead and call."

It took a while for the dispatcher to connect with the sheriff. "Van Horn."

"Sheriff, this is Doug Fletcher, the Park Service investigator. I'd like to meet with you regarding the anchor murder. If there's someone from the county attorney's office available, it would be good to have them in the meeting also."

"You make it sound like you've made some progress."

"I'd prefer to speak in person rather than on a cell phone. But, yes, we have some news."

"I've got some time this morning if you can come into town."

"We're about halfway there."

"Okay. I'll call the courthouse to see if I can find an attorney who's not tied up."

"Great, we should be there in..." I looked at Everett.

"Ten minutes."

"Let's say twenty minutes." I ended the call. "We're going to pick up coffee."

"Really? They have a coffee machine."

"Exactly why we're bringing good coffee with us."

Everett double-parked in front of a downtown café, and I dashed in. Vic English waved as I rushed to the cash register. After ordering four cups of coffee and half a dozen doughnuts to go, Vic approached me.

"Are you buttering up the firemen, so they'll make another dive with you? Did you make an identification from the bones you recovered?"

Every time I'd spoken with Vic, I'd felt like I was being interrogated. It gave me a creepy feeling. "The ME doesn't think there's enough DNA in the bones to attempt a genetic match. We really need to find the skull so we can try for a dental match," I lied.

"Did the fire department or DNR find anything on their sonar? I'd think maybe a skull might show up on the bottom of the lake."

"I'm not aware of anything," I replied as the cashier appeared with my purchase. After paying, I lifted the bag. "Peace offering for the sheriff. He's pissed that I haven't been keeping him updated."

"Tell Dutch to keep his shirt on. This cold case is over thirty years old. He doesn't need to solve it this week."

"Exactly," I said as I carried the bag to the door.

"Was that Vic?" Everett asked as he pulled away.

"Yeah, he wanted an update."

"Did you tell him about Max Davidson's story?"

"Everett, Vic doesn't have a need to know. As a matter of fact, the less Vic knows, the better. He can read about it in the newspaper with everyone else."

"Do you have a problem with Vic?"

"He's asking too many questions. Retired cops know we don't comment on investigations; they respect confidentiality. Vic's way off base."

"I think he's harmless."

"If he's harmless, we don't need to tell him anything."

Arriving at our destination, a sergeant led us to the sheriff's office, where a heavyset young man wearing a tie was talking to Van Horn. I set the bag on Van Horn's desk and opened the top. "Are either of you interested in a brewed cup of coffee and a roll?"

The young man glanced at the sheriff, then at me. "I take it you've tasted the sheriff's office coffee?" He accepted a cup and introduced himself, "I'm Mark Hamline, an assistant county attorney. Dutch asked me to sit in on our meeting."

"Thanks for coming over," I said as I opened the box of doughnuts. "Help yourselves."

Van Horn accepted the coffee but declined the doughnut offer, patting his stomach. "My doctor advised me to cut out all sweets." He closed the door and took the lid off a coffee cup as I took a seat. "Before we get started," the sheriff said, "my people assisted the Border Patrol and the Minnesota DNR with an operation last night. The DNR announced the arrest of Canadian fishermen who strayed into Minnesota waters. Unofficially, we recovered a duffel bag full of drugs."

Everett nodded. "I watched the fireworks from Davidson's dock. Was anyone hurt?"

Van Horn hesitated, then said, "None of my deputies were injured. Let's leave it at that."

Taking the hint to move on, I said, "Mark, we've been investigating the origin of the human leg found attached to the anchor in Rainy Lake. We've had a breakthrough."

Hamline smiled. "Ah, the anchor murder. Vic English said you guys were diving in Black Bay. He was skeptical about your odds of finding anything."

"About Vic..." I paused. "He's sniffing around this like he's still a cop. I'd prefer to share information with only people who have a need to know."

Van Horn nodded. "That's the best suggestion I've ever heard from a federal cop. I'm somewhat surprised that you're here to share your results with us. We have a lot of joint operations with the Border Patrol, but we've been cut out of a lot of operations by the DEA and FBI."

"That's not how Jill and I work." I paused to compose my thoughts. "We think the bones we've recovered belong to a William Flacowski. He's a veteran who worked for Randy Mischke during the summer of 1989. We found a ring with an Army airborne logo. Flacowski was airborne and wore a similar ring."

"That's pretty thin evidence," Van Horn suggested.

"It is. The Duluth ME is attempting to make a DNA match from the bones we've recovered to DNA from an assault case involving Flacowski, while he was stationed in Korea."

Van Horn leaned back and held his cup in both hands. "You've got my attention."

"We spoke with an informant last night who had witnessed an interaction between Flacowski and an underage girl at Davidson's Resort. Based on his observations, he thought Flacowski might've assaulted her."

"Did he know who the girl was?" Hamline asked.

"The victim was Randy Mischke's daughter, Belinda. She was fifteen at the time."

Van Horn whistled. "Have you been able to corroborate that story with the woman?"

"Jill is trying to locate Belinda Mischke."

Hamline set aside his coffee and removed a legal pad from his briefcase. "You said this Flacowski worked for Mischke's machine shop. It was the owner's daughter who was allegedly assaulted by Flacowski?"

"Correct. As for corroboration, we spoke with Max Davidson this morning. He also witnessed the exchange between Flacowski and Belinda. Max and Belinda were close, sort of dating. Something major happened, and Belinda wouldn't talk about it or interact with him at all. He remembered her going on a motorcycle ride with someone who called himself Flacowski, and returning with smudges on her face and leaves stuck on her clothes."

Van Horn sighed. "Shit. I don't suppose anyone thought to take her to the hospital to be examined."

"I don't think so. I assume she was so traumatized by the incident that she chose to hide it from everyone."

Hamline was furiously making notes. "Okay. We think Flacowski assaulted the Mischke girl. We also believe Flacowski is at the bottom of the lake."

"Right," I replied. "And there are a couple more pieces that came out of our conversation with Max Davidson. He remembers being sent out with his dad to search for Mischke's missing boat the next day. Mischke claimed it had been stolen or broken free in the storm the night before. However, when they found the boat, its anchor was missing and so was the rope."

"And the foot had an anchor tied to it," Van Horn said.

"Mischke's anchor was tied to it. The anchor had his initials, RM, welded onto it. He made a big deal about the anchor being missing when Davidsons returned the boat. Max Davidson remembered this morning that the boat was missing the anchor AND the anchor rope. The boat hadn't broken free. It had been untied, and the rope was possibly used to tie up the victim or was dropped overboard with the anchor."

Hamline leaned back. "But Mischke said the boat had been stolen. A thief would've untied it from the dock when he stole it."

I leaned toward Everett, who'd been listening quietly. "Ev, pull up the anchor pictures on your phone." As Everett searched for the pictures, I said, "We know Mischke had motive and opportunity."

"The anchor and rope have been in the water for decades. There's nothing that will connect Mischke directly to Flacowski," Van Horn summarized.

Everett handed me his phone, and I stood so I could show the pictures to the sheriff and assistant county attorney. "This is a picture of the anchor. Look at the knot attaching the rope to the anchor."

"Okay," Van Horn said. "What about it?"

"That's the knot an experienced sailor uses to tie his anchor on. I assume Mischke tied that knot when he bought the anchor. Notice how it makes two loops around the anchor, then is tied off in a figure eight."

"Okay," Hamline said.

I moved to another picture. "This is the knot the killer used to tie the anchor to Flacowski's leg. It's the same, complicated knot."

Hamline smiled and shook his head. "You're stretching."

"We looked at every knot tying up every boat and anchor at Davidson's Resort. Most fishermen aren't skilled at tying knots. We found quite a few half hitches, a clove hitch, and several granny knots. NO ONE had tied an anchor hitch. Not even the people working at the resort."

"We're still dealing with a lot of speculation," Hamline protested.

"I want a search warrant for Mischke's shop, house, garage, and property."

Hamline frowned and looked at Van Horn. "What evidence could you possibly find from a 1989 murder?"

"Flacowski's motorcycle."

Van Horn leaned back. "Why would he keep the guy's motorcycle?"

"It's a valuable piece of machinery, and Mischke is a machinist. I doubt the motorcycle is intact. I'm betting the stripped frame is sitting behind his workshop, or somewhere on his property. If we're lucky, it has a license plate on it."

Van Horn looked at Hamline. "Do you think you could sell a judge on that?"

Hamline stared out of the window. "Draft a warrant. I'll talk to Mary Perpich's clerk. She's usually able to follow a trail of breadcrumbs and is always happy to tie up a sexual assault."

I'd been ignoring my vibrating phone. As Hamline packed up his notes, I checked my caller log. There were several calls from Jill, followed by a text message. *Belinda Mischke Carlson lives in Cotton, Minnesota. I've got her address and phone number.*

"My partner has located Belinda Mischke in Cotton. How far away is that?"

Van Horn looked at Hamline. "What do you think, Mark? It's about two hours?"

I stood and tapped Everett's shoulder. "How long with lights and siren?"

Van Horn laughed. "Mark, are you up for a road trip?"

"I've got..." Hamline closed his eyes. "What the hell. Give me fifteen minutes to talk to the judge's clerk and to move around everything on today's schedule."

The sheriff walked to his door. "I'll have a search warrant for the Mischke place when you return."

"Get a search team set up for tomorrow," I said as we left.

"Are you going to sit with the daughter overnight?" Van Horn asked, "Or, do you have some other plan to keep her from speaking to her parents?"

"Unless I'm mistaken, she's already not speaking to them."

I called Jill as Everett pulled the pickup to the front of the courthouse. "We're on our way to Cotton."

"Not without me!"

"I think it's about a half hour detour to pick you up on the drive to Cotton."

"I don't care if it takes you half a day."

"See if Max will drive you to the highway. We'll pick you up there."

"I think Laney is through with the breakfast rush. Maybe she'll drive me."

I met Hamline on the courthouse steps. "What did the judge's clerk say?" I asked as we hustled to the Park Service pickup.

"The judge has a noon break. If Dutch has the warrant ready, the clerk will present it to the judge then. She didn't think there would be any issue getting the judge to sign it. By the way, I called the St. Louis County Attorney to inform him that we were going to interview a material witness in a Koochiching County murder. He thanked me for the heads up but isn't interested in sending anyone to Cotton to sit in on the interview. He requested that we advise him if we make an arrest and plan to book anyone into their county jail."

"Ah, jurisdictional issues. Being a fed, I seem to step on toes over county and city boundaries. If I arrest Belinda, she'll be my prisoner. We're allowed to deliver our detainees to whichever secure facility is convenient. Since the murder occurred in a township outside of International Falls, I'd choose your county jail."

"I'd still owe the St. Louis County Attorney a courtesy call. If there's a pissing match between the two sheriffs' departments, I'll let you be the moderator."

"No problem. I'll probably be back in Texas before the pissing starts. I'll let my boss sort it out. He lives in Utah and will probably be polite but won't care either."

Hamline shook his head. "It must be nice to be a fed and above all of the local politics."

I let Hamline ride up front with Everett. From the back, I called Jill. "Do you have a ride to the highway?"

"Laney is getting her keys from the cabin. We'll be on the road momentarily."

"Do you know if Belinda has a job or if we can catch her at home?"

"Not yet. I may be able to find something as we drive to Cotton."

"Good luck with that," Hamline said. "We'll get cell phone coverage for about three-quarters of the trip."

"Call her house. Use your superior diplomatic skills to talk her into meeting with us in about two hours."

"Don't you want to surprise her?"

"I don't want to drive two hours to find out that she's driven to Duluth or International Falls for the day."

"Laney is here. We'll be waiting for you on the highway."

Hamline turned to me and said, "Your partner sounds like a spitfire."

Everett snorted. "He's married to his partner. And she's more like a mother than a spitfire."

"Do not say that to Jill," I warned.

"She likes me. I'm sure she'd be flattered to know I think of her as motherly."

"I wouldn't count on that."

Hamline ended our discussion of Jill by asking, "Where's home, Doug?"

"I'm originally from Minnesota. We're based in Texas."

"It seems odd that the Park Service would send you to investigate a cold case like this."

"Because the foot was just discovered, the crime shows up as new on our database."

"Tell me about your confidential informant and conversation with Max Davidson."

"Our informant is a former resort employee. We met him in the dining room. Because he's got local historical knowledge, we asked him a lot of questions. At some point, Jill found the right question, and we got a deluge of information about Will

Flacowski and his activities around the resort."

"And that led to your interview with Max Davidson?"

"Right. Our informant said Davidson was a second witness to the confrontation between Belinda Mischke and Will Flacowski."

"Each of them told you the same story about Belinda and Flacowski?"

"Yes. Because she and Max Davidson were friends, he had a deeper understanding of Belinda and what happened."

"No one has spoken with Belinda about that day?"

"Not to the best of our knowledge. We'd been under the assumption that Flacowski had some sort of issue with an unknown young woman. Until last night, we assumed it was someone who owned a cabin here, or who'd been vacationing in a rental."

"Guys," Everett said, "I see Laney's car."

We rolled to a stop, and Jill climbed in beside me. Laney went to Everett's window. "When will you be back?"

"I don't know."

Laney sighed. "Jill couldn't tell me anything about what you're doing."

Everett nodded, then Laney stepped onto the running board, stuck her head into the cab, and kissed him. "Be safe."

Hamline chuckled. "I remember when my wife and I used to be like that. Now she says, 'don't rush back.'" Hamline turned and introduced himself to Jill. Nodding to her sling, he asked, "What happened to you?"

Jill pulled the sling over her head and crumpled it up. "My shoulder is fine. Just fine. I hope this isn't a wild goose chase."

"Cotton isn't that big. If our party isn't home, I'm sure a neighbor or someone in town will know where to find her."

Jill took out her phone, checked for service, then shushed us. "I'll give her a call."

We rode silently while waiting for the phone to connect, then for the woman to answer. Jill left a message on her voicemail.

"Call the bar," Hamline suggested. "It's probably the hub of the community."

Jill searched for a phone number and said, "I thought that would be the Lutheran church."

"That would've been my second choice."

Jill signaled for quiet. "Hi, I'm trying to find Belinda Carlson." Jill laughed at what the bartender said, then replied, "No, I'm not a bill collector or a cop."

After disconnecting, Jill smiled. "Good call, Hamline. They knew that Belinda Carlson is the school secretary." After a second of searching on her phone, Jill had the school's address.

* * *

Cotton was small. It took no time to find the school. Everett parked in a loading zone and waited with the pickup while Jill, Hamline, and I walked to the front door.

"I prefer that you two take the lead," Hamline suggested. "People sometimes get nervous when they find out I'm a county attorney."

"More so than when they find out Jill and I are federal cops?"

"You'd be surprised at the animosity people feel toward lawyers."

A middle-aged woman with gray roots in her brown hair looked up when the door opened. If she was surprised to see three people walking in, two who were wearing badges, she didn't show it. "Good morning," she said, smiling.

"Are you Belinda Carlson?" Jill asked.

"I am. How can I help you?"

Jill held up her credentials. "I'm a federal law enforcement officer. Is there somewhere we could talk privately?"

"Federal? Is Mike okay?"

"Your family is fine. We need to ask you some questions about an investigation."

A man's head popped out from a door behind the reception desk. "Is everything okay, Belle?"

"Um, yeah. Could you watch the desk for a minute? I need to show these people to the media room."

Carlson led us down a hallway and unlocked a room. "I think this will be okay."

The room was set up with televisions, movie projectors, and recording devices.

Carlson closed the door and leaned against it as if she were blocking our exit. "What's this about?"

Jill stepped forward and handed Carlson her business card. "We're investigating a body that was found in Voyageurs National Park. I hope you can help us by answering some quick questions."

Carlson looked past Jill at Hamline and me. "Who are they?"

"Doug is my partner, and Mr. Hamline is the assistant county attorney."

Carlson nodded. "How can *I* help? I haven't lived up north for years."

"We found Will Flacowski's body."

Carlson blinked but didn't respond.

"You were one of the last people to see him alive."

"I doubt that. Will was very popular, and I hardly knew him."

"We know he assaulted you."

Carlson's professional façade cracked. "I don't know what you're talking about." She turned to open the door, but Jill stopped her.

"We interviewed Max Davidson this morning."

Carlson huffed. "Max outed me?"

"He was your friend. He still cares about you."

"I sincerely doubt Max, or anyone else in I-Falls has thought about me in thirty years."

"What happened when your father found out about the assault?"

"Assault?"

"We know Will Flacowski raped you during a motorcycle ride. Is that when your father dealt with Will?"

Belinda shook her head emphatically. "Dad was having problems with Will's work. He fired him."

"We found Will's body tied to your father's anchor on the bottom of Black Bay."

That news stunned Carlson. After a pause, she replied, "Dad's anchor disappeared when his boat was stolen."

Jill glanced at me. "Belinda, your father tied the anchor to Will's foot and threw him overboard."

"You don't know that!" she replied, too quickly.

"We do know that. We also know he returned to the dock, then set his boat adrift during a storm. He told the neighbors it had blown away and asked them to help find it. The problem we have is, there was no way for your father to secure the boat because the rope was tied to Flacowski and the anchor."

"The boat was stolen."

"Someone would have to drive up your driveway and walk past the house to get to the boat. That didn't happen, did it?"

Belinda hung her head.

"Mrs. Carlson," Hamline said, "If you cooperate with us, I'm prepared to offer immunity in return for your cooperation and testimony."

"I can't testify against my father."

Discerning Belinda's comment, Jill put her hand on Carlson's arm. "Just tell us what happened that night."

"I can't. I can't tell you. I can't tell anyone," Carlson sobbed.

I found a box of tissues on a shelf near a DVD player and handed a few to Carlson.

"Mrs. Carlson, I'm afraid we'll have to bring you back to International Falls for formal questioning as a material witness to Will Flacowski's murder," Hamline explained.

"You don't understand," Carlson wailed.

"Help us to understand," Jill said softly. "What did your father do to Will Flacowski?"

"My father didn't do anything to Will."

"What happened?" Jill asked.

Carlson turned her head away and stared into the corner. "I killed him."

"You killed him?" I asked, not believing her statement.

She nodded.

Trying to unveil her lie, I asked, "How did you kill him?"

She turned her head toward me. "How?"

"Did you stab him with a butcher knife? Feed him rat poison? Cut off his head with an ax?"

She hesitated a second too long before replying, "I blew his head off with a shotgun. Dad just disposed of the body."

Jill turned to me and shook her head and mouthed, *she's lying.*

Hamline stepped forward and asked, "Mrs. Carlson, where is the shotgun you used?"

"I don't know. I suppose I threw it...into the lake."

"Where was Mr. Flacowski when you shot him? Did this happen on your family property or somewhere else?"

"Will and my dad were arguing on the dock. I shot him to stop the fight."

"Where did you get the shotgun?" Hamline asked, "Was it Will's gun? Your dad's?"

"I...don't remember."

An idea struck me, and I said, "We'll have to give you a lie detector test. There's an excellent guy in Duluth. He's about ninety-nine-point-nine percent correct."

"Why do I have to take a lie detector test? I've admitted to killing Will."

"It's a formality," I explained. "The jury will want to have that evidence."

"I'll plead guilty. There won't be a trial."

"Your father won't let you plead guilty for something he did," Jill said softly.

"He didn't kill Will. I told you, I did it."

"Your father will set the record straight. He won't let you go to prison for his crime. We know he's an angry man. It's easy to see how he would lash out after discovering that Will raped you."

"Please, go," Belinda sobbed. "Everyone in town is going to find out I rode off on Will's motorcycle. They'll all say, 'What a stupid girl. Riding away with a guy twenty years older. She was asking for it.'"

"It wasn't your fault," Jill replied softly. "You weren't 'asking for it.' Will violated you against your will."

"Yeah, right. I wasn't smart enough to know what I was getting myself into. Not smart enough to hide the pregnancy."

I saw Jill grimace at the announcement of the pregnancy. "Did you keep the baby?"

Carlson nodded. "My husband is a saint for marrying a twenty-year-old woman with a four-year-old kid. My husband's a pharmacist in Duluth."

"Your son won't believe his mother is a murderer. You need to be there for him and your grandchildren."

Carlson sobbed. "My grandchildren."

"They've never met your father, have they?" Jill asked.

"No."

"You didn't want them to know the murderer who raised you."

"I told you, it wasn't my father!"

Hamline said, "I'm going to ask the officers to arrest you and read you your rights. You don't need to say anything more without having an attorney present."

"Please don't handcuff me inside the school. I don't want the children to see me being led away in cuffs."

Jill took Carlson's elbow and led her out of the media room. I kept Hamline behind after they left. "I don't think her father did it."

"I don't think Belinda did it either. Who does that leave besides her father? Her mother? Karl Peterson? Max Davidson? Lyle Sertich?"

"Let's execute the search warrant tomorrow and question Mr. and Mrs. Mischke."

"Okay. But neither of them can testify against the other. We might not get anywhere." Hamline opined. He took out his cell phone. "I'm going to call the St. Louis County Attorney to let him know we've made an arrest."

"Can you wait until we get back to I-Falls? I'd like to get a good night's rest before the irate calls start."

Hamline shook his head. "You really don't care about our county boundaries, do you?"

"It's not that I don't care. I don't like dotted lines on a map defining how I pursue a case."

"It must be nice," Hamline replied as he placed the call.

# Chapter 15

We booked Belinda into the Koochiching County Jail, where we were met by Sheriff Van Horn and a sergeant he introduced as Rod Poquette. "I've got a search warrant for Mischke's. Rod has a team lined up for eight tomorrow morning."

Poquette looked about thirty, was trim and could've been on a sheriff's department recruiting poster. "How many of you are planning to search with us?"

"All three of us," I replied, pointing to Jill, Everett, and myself.

"We're planning to gather here at the courthouse. I've got a female deputy to detain Mrs. Mischke, and Dutch knows Randy Mischke, so he's going to stick with him. I figured two people in the house, two people in the shop, and two or three walking the property. The warrant includes computers, cell phones, financial records, business records, firearms, human remains, and motor vehicles on the warrant. Dutch said you had something specific in mind?"

"The victim was seen riding a motorcycle around the area in the days before he disappeared. I hope we'll find at least the frame or engine somewhere in the shop or on the property."

Jill spoke up. "You have human remains on the warrant? We found the victim's bones across the lake. Do you expect to find additional victims buried on the property?"

Poquette looked at the sheriff. "Mischke is a hot head, and this Flacowski isn't the only open missing person case. If Randy killed off Flacowski for...whatever, he might've done the same thing to others."

"Ah," I said. "Like Vic English's story about following a blood trail from the motel."

Van Horn stared at me as if weighing his answer. "I know Vic has retold that story a thousand times. There isn't a single police report about an investigation into that scenario."

"It was a city police investigation," I suggested.

"Our departments share the space, jail, and a record system. There is no case anywhere but in Vic's head."

Poquette listened intently to the discussion, then addressed us. "I've told my search team not to discuss this search with anyone else. I assume the three of you aren't planning to talk to Vic about it over a cup of coffee."

I shook my head. "I totally agree. This is on a need-to-know basis. Vic doesn't need to know."

"Are you meeting us in town, or at the end of the road to Mischke's?"

"Let's meet at the end of the road," I suggested.

"If you're planning to be part of the property search, I suggest that you wear boots. About half of Mischke's land is swamp. Boots will also help keep the ticks off of you. You'll need bug spray for the mosquitoes."

Jill looked at me. "I'll stay with the group in the shop."

Everett shrugged. "I can walk the swamp."

Van Horn looked at me, then smiled. "Rod, you should probably pick your younger deputies to walk the swamp. It might be tough on someone Doug's age."

I chuckled. "As much as that's an ageist comment, I'm not going to argue with the sentiment. My swamp slogging days are over."

* * *

I knocked on Max Davidson's office door. "Come in."

Davidson was facing his computer which showed a huge spreadsheet. He nodded toward the numbers. "Everyone thinks owning a resort is a dream job." He shut off the monitor and turned to me. "Sometimes it's more of a nightmare than a dream."

"I'd like to talk to Karl Peterson again. We can walk to his cabin if you'll call to let him know we're coming."

Max snorted. "I haven't been in Karl's cabin in a couple of decades. I suggest you meet him over here."

"It's that bad?" Jill asked.

"Imagine a house where a toothless hermit has lived alone since his wife died twenty years ago. Oh, and he's a bit of a hoarder, so you have to work your way through the maze of boxes, catalogs, books, magazines and TV dinner trays."

Jill grimaced. "Do you mind if we meet with him here?"

Max opened a cabinet and took out a bottle of blackberry brandy. From a different cabinet, he removed four lowball glasses with the resort logo printed on them. "I have a good time talking to Karl. If you don't mind my sitting in on your discussion. I could leave if you want to..."

I cut off Max's comment. "If you don't mind, we'd like to talk to Karl alone."

"No problem. I need to check with housekeeping. We have a washer down and the repairman was supposed to be here this afternoon."

Davidson walked away and Jill looked at the bottle of brandy. "Without Davidson drinking, this bottle is going to last a long time."

"We'll send Karl home with it."

A moment later, Karl walked in with his stench preceding him. He looked around. "Where's Max?"

"He was called away," Jill said. "But he left a bottle of brandy out." She slid the bottle and one glass to Karl.

Without hesitation, Karl unscrewed the cap and poured until the glass was nearly full. I guessed he'd poured nearly eight ounces of liquor. Suddenly aware that we didn't have any brandy, he pulled two glasses over and started pouring.

"None for me," I said, putting my hand over the glass.

"Suit yourself," he said as he slid a nearly overflowing glass to Jill. He lifted his glass in a toast, spilling a little on Max's desk. "Skol!"

Jill slid the glass in front of her, took a tiny sip. She stifled a cough, but not the accompanying gasp.

"We learned some more about the guy who was tied to the anchor. His name was Will Flaco or Flacowski. You remember him, don't you?"

Karl wasn't a poker player and his attempt to hide his reaction was half-hearted. "Never heard of him."

"You had a pushing match with him here at the resort after he brought back Mischke's daughter from a motorcycle ride."

Realizing he'd been caught in a lie, Karl drank the remaining brandy in one swallow. I expected him to walk away. Instead, he poured himself another glassful. "What of it?"

"What happened after that?"

"I suppose he rode his motorbike off."

Jill leaned forward. "You knew what happened to Belinda Mischke on that motorcycle ride."

"I didn't *know* anything."

"But you suspected something had happened or you wouldn't have confronted Flacowski."

Karl stared at his glass, then drank the last half. "I've seen lots of things over the years. You know how it goes. There are people breaking laws all the time. I don't call the game warden because I see a guy with two limits of walleyes. I don't call the cops because I see a guy driving drunk. It's none of my damn business what other people do." Karl poured himself another glass of blackberry brandy, which lowered the bottle to half, or less.

I was about to go *bad cop* on Karl when Jill put her hand on my arm. She leaned forward and took a sip of brandy, apparently signaling their bonding, or something. "Belinda was attacked. Made to do something she fought back against. You knew Flacowski was a jerk, capable of hurting a girl like her. You confronted him."

Karl's head wobbled, but he didn't look up. "I probably told him he was a shit and that was the end of it."

"Was that the end of it?"

Karl's eyes looked up, and he stared at Jill through his bushy eyebrows. "What are you accusing me of?"

"I'm not accusing you of anything. I'm just asking if you said or did anything more to Flacowski after he rode away."

Karl shook his head.

"Flacowski died shortly after that. Do you know anything more?"

"She wasn't the first," he mumbled.

"Who wasn't the first?"

"The Mischke girl."

"Flacowski attacked another girl?"

"Probably. Shits like him don't start attacking girls when they're thirty years old. He was a predator. Period. He got what he deserved." Karl stood and grabbed the brandy bottle by the neck. "I'm taking the rest of this home."

"Were you the one who gave him what he deserved?" I asked.

"I wish it had been me."

"Do you know who drowned him?" I asked.

"Flacowski didn't drown," he muttered. Then, he stumbled out of the office.

"What happened?" I asked.

Karl waved his arm as he walked away, signaling the end of his interview.

"He knows Flacowski was dead before he was dumped in the lake," Jill observed.

"I'm not convinced of that. He's heard that, so he thinks he knows it."

"Who would've told him?" As soon as the words were out of Jill's mouth, she tipped her head back. "Vic."

"Or any of a hundred other characters in town who've speculated on what happened to Flacowski."

Max Davidson stuck his head into the office. "Karl's gone? Are you through?"

"Karl said Flacowski was dead before he was dumped in the lake. Do you know if he knows that? Or does he believe it because people have talked about it?" I asked.

"With Karl, it's hard to tell. He's embellished so many tall tales it's hard to parse fiction from the truth."

"Do you think Karl could've killed Flacowski?" Jill asked.

"Even back in the day, Karl was a drinker, not a fighter. There's no way he could've killed Flacowski."

"Does Karl own guns?"

"He's sold everything he owned to buy booze."

"He still has a cabin," I countered.

"I own the cabin. He'll live there as long as he wants. When he dies, I'll probably burn the place down and build something new."

"Doesn't he scare off your customers?"

Snorting, Max replied, "You'd be surprised how many people come back asking about the grisly, toothless storyteller. He's part of the rustic resort experience." Davidson paused. "I know he's a drunk, but he's a happy drunk. And he's not going to do anything other than spin another tall tale that'll have people laughing about him long after they've left the resort."

Davidson saw my look of skepticism. "Karl and Lyle are part of the fabric of this resort as much as the walleye on the menu. Coming to a resort isn't just fishing. It's an experience of life beyond what you live at home. People expect to see knotty pine paneling, mounted fish, and colorful people. One of the resorts used to pay Bronco Nagurski to drink at their bar. The place would be packed on the nights Bronco was there telling his football and wrestling stories. I'm sure there are people who tell their grandchildren they remember meeting Bronco Nagurski from International Falls, one of the original inductees in the NFL Hall of Fame."

"I've got to say, Karl and Lyle are colorful, but they aren't the draw of someone like Bronco."

Max nodded toward his door. "Look at the framed pictures and newspaper articles in the dining room and bait shop. Karl and Lyle are our fishing hall of fame. When Karl starts talking about stringers of twelve-pound walleyes and his world-record walleye, he's talking from experience. He'll show you the pictures."

We thanked Max and walked to his door. Jill paused and asked, "Isn't Tammy Fae Baker, the queen of heavy makeup, from International Falls?"

Laughing, Max said, "Shh. And don't tell anyone my dad dated her when they were in high school."

When we were well away from Davidson's office, Jill asked, "What do you think about Davidson's claim that Karl is harmless?"

I pointed to a row of pictures mounted alongside the fireplace. We walked over and saw a younger Karl Peterson, bare chested with arms as big around as my thighs, holding a pair of Northern Pike that had to weigh twenty-five pounds each. The next picture was of Karl holding a stringer of walleyes that had to weigh close to eighty pounds.

"Flacowski was killed over three decades ago. Back then, Karl could've snapped Flacowski's neck like a toothpick."

"And he says Flacowski was dead before he went into the lake," Jill quoted.

* * *

The lodge restaurant was quieter than it had been on previous evenings. We ate in silence because there were too many people there who might overhear our conversation about the case weighing heavily on our minds.

We were waiting for our bill when Booger/Lyle walked into the bar. He was focused on his favorite bar stool and was nearly past us before he looked up and saw Jill. He paused, smiled, then walked over to our table. "You talked to Max this morning."

I glanced around and noticed two people who looked our way after they heard the owner's name mentioned. "Jill, why don't you take Lyle outside to talk about whatever he may have remembered since we spoke last night."

Lyle frowned. "I ain't got nothin' new. I was just wondering…"

Jill stood and put her hand on Lyle's arm. "Let's talk outside, Lyle."

Lyle's reluctance evaporated when Jill touched his arm. She led him outside like a puppy following its master.

Megan arrived with our check. I added a reasonable tip and charged it to our room. She nodded toward the door. "You'd better keep an eye on Jill. Booger is smitten."

"I'm confident Jill will return to our cabin with me." As an afterthought, I pulled $20 from my wallet and handed it to Megan. "Treat Lyle to whatever he wants tonight."

Megan fingered the money. "This is too much. If Booger drank this much beer, someone would have to carry him home, and it wouldn't be me."

"Put it on his tab and let him drink it off over a couple of nights."

Megan leaned close to me and whispered, "I'm not supposed to know this; Booger drinks for free."

"Why?"

"Mr. Davidson told me Booger and his father were high school friends. I guess Booger was a mess after Vietnam and his divorce, so Max's dad gave Booger a job as a guide and let him stay year-round in one of the cabins. Booger never betrayed that kindness and was the resort handyman, fishing guide, and storyteller for nearly all his life. In his last days, Mr. Davidson Senior told Max that Booger was to be treated like his uncle. Booger's retirement is free room, board, and a couple of beers a night."

"Wow, that's the kind of loyalty to a friend you don't often see."

Megan nodded. "As much as we kid about Booger, he's a kindly old guy who has never said a harsh word or made an inappropriate move on any of us." She paused. "Those of us who've been around a couple of years have been treated like family by the Davidsons. In return, we are happy to come back here year after year."

"Not many people can say that about their jobs."

"There is nothing any of us would do to tarnish the resort's reputation or betray Mr. and Mrs. Davidson's trust."

"How do you feel about Mischkes?"

Megan stared at me, biting her lip. "My mother told me I shouldn't say anything if I couldn't say something good about a person." She turned and walked away.

I found Jill and Lyle standing under a yard light having a conversation and swatting mosquitoes while a lonely loon called in the distance. "If you moved away from the light, there might be fewer mosquitoes," I suggested.

"That's an old wives' tale," Lyle said. "They're attracted to the carbon dioxide in your breath."

Impressed by that tidbit, I asked, "Really?"

Booger shrugged. "I guided for a university professor who told me that. He said that's how the buggers can even find you in the dark."

"Do you have a tick repellent theory?" I asked.

Booger frowned. "It's best if you stay out of the long grass. I've never got a tick walking on a gravel road."

"I heard you've been working at the resort since you came back from 'Nam."

Booger nodded without reply.

I put out my hand. "Thanks for your service."

Reluctantly, he shook my hand. His grip seemed frail and unsteady. "Nobody said that when we came home. Max's dad was the only one who even bought me a drink."

"I heard he gave you a job."

Lyle shook his head. "He saved my life." With that comment, he walked away to get his evening beer.

"What was that about?" Jill asked.

"Lyle's been working and living here since he got out of the Army. Max was told to treat him like an old uncle."

"Like my Uncle Chet," Jill suggested.

"Exactly. What did he have to say?"

"He knew we'd talked to Max and wanted to know if what he'd told us was helpful. I said it was, and that we'd made an arrest."

"I hope you assured him that we appreciated his help."

"He asked me if we'd arrested Randy Mischke. I told him Mischke was a person of interest."

"Lyle accepted that?"

"Not entirely, he told me Randy wasn't the person who killed Flacowski."

"Did you mention Karl as a murder suspect?"

"Karl didn't kill Flacowski. He minds his own business."

"Booger may be right. Belinda admitted to the murder."

"I have the impression Lyle may know more than he's told us. I don't think he'll *tell us* anything more. But he might expand on something we know if the right question is asked."

I gestured toward the path to our cabin. "You're talking in riddles, and it's been a long day."

Jill slipped into the cabin quickly and swatted the mosquitoes that came in with us.

"I'm going to take a shower. Check yourself for ticks."

She disappeared into the bathroom, and I called after her. "It'd be more interesting to have you check me for ticks."

"We've already had that discussion. It's not happening." A second later, the shower water started running.

I found a tick crawling up my leg. In the process of flicking it out the door, I let in a few more mosquitoes. *This brings back memories of Scout camp,* I thought to myself.

# Chapter 16

Everett met us for breakfast the next morning. Laney seemed even more attentive than she had been previously. When she left to pick up an order for a neighboring table, I commented, "You two seem to be getting along well."

"Almost too well. I think her college boyfriend was abusive. Last night, she told me she's afraid he'll show up at the resort."

I looked at Jill. "Did you get that sense when she drove you out to the road where we picked you up?"

"Our discussion was limited to which classes a person should take if they're going to be a park ranger, followed by my job history."

Everett nodded. "Laney's goals are shifting."

After delivering plates to the table next to us, Laney topped off our coffee and sat at our fourth chair. "Ev's been really secretive. He wouldn't tell me about what happened after you picked up Jill. And he's not sharing what's happening today."

I nodded and zipped my lips.

Jill rolled her eyes. "Our investigation is at a critical point. We can't discuss what's going on."

"You guys really can keep secrets."

"It's part of our job description," I replied. "Investigate crimes and keep secrets."

Laney glanced at the people sitting at the other two occupied tables. Seeing they were busy eating, she leaned close to Jill. "Can I talk to you for a second?"

"Sure," Jill replied as she stood. Together, she and Laney walked outside.

"What's that about?" I asked.

Everett frowned. "I don't know. I said talking to Jill was kind of like talking to my mom without judgment and guilt."

I laughed. "Hmm. That's not what being married to her is like. There's lots of judgment, although not too much guilt."

Laney returned, smiling at us, then checking on the other diners before disappearing into the kitchen. Jill looked less happy. "Where is Laney going to college?"

"Minnesota State Mankato. Why?"

Jill didn't answer. She turned to me. "What county is Mankato in?"

"I skipped that day of Minnesota geography."

Looking less than pleased with that reply, Jill walked back outside.

"I wonder what that's about?" Everett asked.

Laney returned with the bill, which I signed. She pecked Everett's cheek. "Be safe."

"Sure," he replied.

Jill was leaning against the pickup's fender talking on the phone. She walked away from us as we approached. Catching the hint, I nodded toward our cabin. "I doubt we'll need them, but let's get the bulletproof vests from our cabin."

Everett looked back toward Jill. "What's she up to?"

"She's probably talking to her cousin about her Uncle Chet's prostate issues."

"She talks to her cousin about her uncle's prostate?"

"It's a long story."

Jill was off the phone when we returned to the pickup. She nodded toward the back bumper and told Everett we'd get in the truck in a minute.

"What did Susie say about Chet's prostate?" I asked for Everett's benefit as he got into the driver's seat and closed the door.

"What?"

"I told Everett you were checking on Chet's prostate issues."

"Yuck? Why'd you tell him that?"

"Because I knew that would send him away, and I didn't want to tell him you were calling the Mankato Police Department to report an abuse situation."

Jill sighed. "Laney has been..."

I put up my hand. "I don't need details because I can read your body language. What did they say?"

"Her asshole boyfriend has protective orders against him from two previous relationships. He's on probation for an assault and has two DUI convictions. I told them Laney was afraid he was going to drive up and hurt her, or worse. The officer I spoke with said that it was unlikely. His license restrictions from his last DUI only allow him to drive to work and the grocery store. They're going to check on him and remind him of his driving restrictions."

"Great," I said as I reached for the pickup door.

Jill held the door shut. "Laney doesn't want to go back to Mankato."

"It's not our call. She's a big girl capable of making her own arrangements."

"I want to talk to Max Davidson tonight."

Reading Jill's mind, I said, "I don't know that he's ready to take on more charity cases like Lyle and Karl."

"This one isn't going to be another lifetime commitment. Laney will be living with Everett before the end of the summer."

"Is that your judgment or Laney's plan?"

"I may have planted those seeds."

"No wonder Laney thinks you're like Everett's mom."

* * *

We were waiting at the turnoff to Mischke's when the caravan of sheriff's vehicles approached. The lead vehicle flashed its headlights at us, and Everett started the engine. We turned down the road, and then followed them into Mischke's yard, each of us parking at an angle that either blocked vehicles or the driveway.

Van Horn led our group to the front door. He knocked and announced, "Sheriff's Department!"

Randy Mischke had crumbs on his shirt as if we'd caught him eating a piece of toast. "Dutch, what's going on?"

The sheriff pulled open the storm door and handed the search warrant to Mischke. "We have a search warrant for your house, shop, and property." He waved the female deputy into the house, and we heard her talking to Peggy Mischke while Randy Mischke watched in shock.

Poquette dispatched teams to the house and shop. Three deputies returned to their squads to put on rubber hip boots. He turned to us. "Everett, are you still planning to search the property?"

He pointed at his rubber, mid-calf barn boots. "I'm set."

Poquette smiled. "You're planning to only search the shallow swamps?"

Everett hesitated. "Whatever it takes..."

Poquette turned to us. "Jill, you said you'd help with the shop. Doug, you and I can check the area around the outbuildings."

Poquette and I walked to the machine shop building, which was a pole barn about thirty yards away from the house. There were two other storage sheds behind the shop; both had weeds growing in front of their doors, indicating they hadn't been in recent use. The shop's two garage doors facing the driveway were open, and we followed Jill and a deputy into the pole barn. The floor of the 20'x40' building was filled with motors, machine parts, and pieces of metal, apparently awaiting processing by welding, cutting, or machining. A rack along one wall held long steel and aluminum rods and bars. The back of the building was an office with a single entrance. Jill and a deputy stepped into the office while Poquette and I walked through the equipment and work staged on the shop floor, much of it sitting on wooden pallets. Several of the pieces along the wall were rusty, like they'd been discarded or deprioritized, some for years. We walked along the walls, stepping over pallets, chunks of metal, and pieces of wood arranged to keep the metal items from rolling.

Poquette stopped next to a push lawnmower. "Mischke must work on anything from lawn equipment to industrial rollers for the paper mill."

"There's a word for that; eclectic?"

"He's a talented mechanic and machinist who's capable of fixing anything."

"Eclectic."

Poquette glanced at me. "Whatever."

After circling the interior of the shop, we walked outside. At some point in the past, trees had been cleared to build the shop. Mature birch and smaller pine trees grew twenty or thirty feet away from the building. Nearer to the structure, some smaller poplars had sprouted and were now fifteen to twenty feet high. Nearest the building was knee-high green grass growing through a mat of tangled brown grass that hadn't been mown in years. Scattered in the grass were rusty car engines and an old tractor.

"These must be the unrepairable orphans," Poquette opined. "I suppose he set these aside for some future time and he stayed busy enough that they never became a priority."

I walked through the weeds near the building while Poquette walked a few feet farther from the foundation. I stumbled a couple of times, once over an old drive shaft hidden in the grass, the second time over a branch.

Poquette laughed. "Dutch was right when he said you shouldn't be walking the swamp. You might've drowned."

Brushing the dust off my knees after the second fall, I tried to maintain my dignity. "That last branch was well hidden under the matted grass."

Poquette laughed. "Sure. Whatever you say."

Through the underbrush, I caught a glimpse of Everett and the two deputies slogging through a swampy area parallel to us. Beyond them was the shimmering lake. "This has to be a valuable chunk of land. Mischke must own twenty acres, and it's surrounded on three sides by water. I'd think someone would want to build a resort here."

"I think the development along the lake is restricted. Besides, this is his business and home. He probably isn't interested in moving."

The next time I fell, it was a full faceplant. Poquette walked over and helped me to my feet. "Another branch?"

I kicked at the grass. Whatever lay underneath it was solid. "Maybe a rock."

Poquette bent down and pulled the matted grass aside. "You got a pipe this time." He paused. "Hold on. This isn't a pipe."

Together, we pulled the grass aside, slowly uncovering a motorcycle frame. The motor, gas tank, and tires were gone. The seat had been eaten by rodents, and the remaining wires and cables were gnawed or broken. I pushed the grass away from the rear fender and saw something white.

"I've got a license plate."

Poquette helped me uncover the rear fender and the license plate. "The last tabs were put on in 1989."

"Call it in," I suggested.

Using his shoulder-mounted radio, Poquette contacted the dispatcher and requested ownership information on the license plate. While waiting, he took a few pictures of the frame where it lay next to the building. Then, we tipped the motorcycle frame up and leaned it against the siding. A moment later, the dispatcher replied to the information request.

"The owner is William Flacowski. The Honda motorcycle was last registered in 1989. His address is a PO box in Hugo, Minnesota."

"Flacowski," I said. "Shortened to Flaco."

Poquette stepped back and looked at the grimy frame. "I doubt Flacowski left his most prized possession behind."

"Let's walk the rest of the perimeter and then talk to Van Horn."

The sheriff and a female deputy were sitting at the kitchen table with Peggy and Randy Mischke. They all looked up when we walked in. "Are you about through?" Randy asked. "I have a business to run."

"We found Will Flacowski's motorcycle frame behind your shop," I said.

Peggy's head spun, and she glared at her husband. "You kept his motorcycle?"

"Shut up, Peggy," Randy spat. "That doesn't mean anything."

"Belinda is in the county jail. She admitted killing Flacowski," I explained.

Randy closed his eyes and shook his head. "Belinda didn't have anything to do with it."

The female deputy checked a small black recorder set on the table. Apparently, making sure it had captured Peggy's incriminating comment.

A car pulled up outside the house and a door slammed. I was about to ask Randy to explain himself when Vic English walked into the kitchen. "So, this is where all the cops went."

Van Horn stood and pointed at the door. "You've got to leave, Vic."

"Are you kidding? All you'd do by sending me away is delaying the information. I'm going to get the news about this search in the coffee shop anyway."

Poquette walked to Vic and grabbed his elbow, pushing him toward the door. "Leave, Vic."

Vic looked at Randy. "It looks like you need a lawyer. Don't say anything."

As Poquette urged Vic toward the door, Randy said, "Belinda told them she killed Flacowski, Vic. I can't let that stand."

The ex-cop tried to pull himself free from Poquette's grip. "Don't say anything more. Get a lawyer!"

Poquette shoved Vic out of the door and stood on the steps until he was convinced the ex-cop was leaving. He stepped back into the house, shaking his head. "Vic needs to be knocked down a notch. Can we arrest him for obstruction or something?"

Van Horn turned back to Randy Mischke. "Belinda didn't kill Flacowski?"

"God, no," Randy choked out. "She was in the house with Peggy. She's protecting me."

"You killed Flacowski?" Van Horn asked.

Randy shook his head but didn't answer.

A shot from outside the house rattled the kitchen windows, startling all of us. Van Horn and the female deputy rolled off their chairs and took cover below the bottom of the window next to the table. Poquette, who was closest to the kitchen door, drew his pistol and flew out of the door with me a step behind him. Van Horn and the female deputy put their backs against the wall and followed.

Poquette took cover behind Vic's car and scanned the area with his pistol, looking for a threat. I turned in the opposite direction when I exited the house. Looking around the corner of the house, I spotted no activity between the house and the shop. The smell of burnt gunpowder hung in the air, but no one was in sight. Poquette approached Vic's open car door, but shook his head, indicating Vic wasn't in or near the vehicle. The deputies who were searching the swamp yelled and pointed behind the car, but they were still beyond the shop, and I couldn't discern what they were trying to communicate to us. Jill and the deputy, who'd been searching the shop, peeked out of the pole barn door with their pistols drawn.

Van Horn and the female deputy approached me as Poquette reported shots fired and our location.

"Where the hell did Vic go?"

The kitchen window blew out, sending a spray of glass across the lawn. We all took cover. I looked for Poquette, who had been standing next to Vic's car and had been showered with broken glass. His head popped up behind Vic's car, and he signaled that he was unhurt.

I'd taken a step out of the front door when I heard Vic inside the house yelling, "No, Randy. It's not that bad!" A second later, a second muffled shot rattled the windows.

An eerie dog's howl came from inside the house, followed by frantic scratching at the door. When I opened the door, the dog shot past me and flew toward the shop.

I ran into the kitchen with my pistol drawn, but it was clear the shooting was over. Vic knelt next to Randy's body, where he appeared to be removing a shotgun from Randy's hands. Peggy Mischke's face was gone, and the wall around the window was misted with blood and tissue. She lay in a heap on the floor with blood pooling around her. Vic stood behind the table, holding a pump shotgun in his left hand. He looked at me when he sensed motion. "That crazy sonofabitch shot Peggy, and then himself."

I aimed my pistol at Vic. "Set the shotgun down and put your hands behind your head."

"What the hell, Fletcher. It's a murder/suicide."

"Shotgun on the floor. Hands behind your head. Then turn away."

"Jesus Christ, Fletcher. I'm a cop. What the hell are you doing?"

Poquette joined me inside the kitchen, followed by Van Horn. Taking in the scene, the sergeant sucked in her breath and shuddered. Van Horn glanced at Vic, the dead Mischkes, then at me.

"What's going on, Fletcher?"

Without taking my aim off Vic, I asked, "Was there a shotgun in the kitchen when you were talking to Randy and Peggy?"

"No. Why?"

"Vic suckered us into rushing into the yard while he snuck in through the front door with his shotgun. He killed the Mischkes, then placed his shotgun in Randy's hands, hoping we'd believe it was a murder suicide."

Vic shook his head. "No, that's not what happened. Randy had the shotgun…"

"Set the shotgun on the floor, Vic. Hands behind your head. NOW!"

Vic raised his right hand and bent down, setting the shotgun on the floor. With the shotgun down, he raised both hands with his palms towards us, to armpit height. Not behind his head, as I directed.

Van Horn took in the scene and then nodded to me. "Poquette, cuff him and bag his hands. We're going to test for gunshot residue."

"Of course, there's gunshot residue on my hands," Vic protested. "I pulled the shotgun out of Randy's hand to make sure it was safe."

"Where did you shoot Flacowski, Vic?" I asked. "Did you shoot him in the yard? Behind the shop? On the dock? What was your motive? Had he done something in town? Or did you just kill him because he was a lying vet who was charming all the local women?"

"You're going to regret this, Fletcher," Vic said as he lowered his hands. "This is a murder and suicide. You've got no evidence other than what you see."

I nodded to the black recorder on the table. "Listening to what you said to the Mischkes while we were outside should be enlightening."

Vic's eyes darted from me to the recorder and back. I watched his confident façade crumble.

"Keep your hands up, Vic."

"Why? So you can send me to prison? Old cops don't do well in prison."

"Raise your hands, Vic. Keep them where I can see them."

Jill and another deputy joined us in the tiny kitchen, making it crowded. Over my shoulder, I said, "Poquette, you and Jill circle around and block the living room door."

I heard them trot out with Everett a step behind as an ominous grin curled on Vic's lips.

"You've got it all figured out, don't you. What was the tip off?" Vic asked.

"The missing skull."

"Huh. You couldn't just let that remain a mystery. Flacowski's head could be anywhere."

"It's spread across the lake, isn't it, Vic? It was blown to pieces, just like Peggy Mischke's face. Belinda saw you and her father on the dock, maybe from an upstairs window. It was raining, and there were two people on the dock. She assumed her father pulled the trigger, but Randy wasn't that vindictive. Randy wasn't the one who pulled the trigger. It was you. What was your motive? Love? Money? Power?" I paused. "Wait, it was drugs. Flacowski was moving drugs for you. You convinced Randy to hire Flacowski, so he'd have a reason to be here. Flacowski messed it all up when he assaulted Belinda. Randy confronted you about the rape, and Flacowski had to be dealt with. Is that it?"

I heard motion in the living room and asked, "Poquette, can you see if he's got a pistol in a holster or tucked into his waistband behind his back?"

"I can't tell if he's got a gun under his jacket or not."

"Vic, raise your hands and place your fingers behind your head. You're under arrest for the murders of William Flacowski and Randy and Peggy Mischke."

Vic sneered, "No Koochiching County jury will convict me."

"You committed a murder in Voyageurs National Park. You're going to be arraigned in front of a federal magistrate. The Flacowski murder trial will be in Duluth or Minneapolis."

Vic swung his right hand down as he twisted. I was about to snap off a shot when I heard shots from the living room. I hesitated, waiting to see if Vic was incapacitated. Four more shots rang out as Everett and Van Horn fired. Vic doubled over, still reaching for a weapon behind his back. He stumbled, then his legs turned to Jell-O, and he collapsed on top of Randy Mischke. I glanced to my right and saw Van Horn aiming over the table, preparing for another shot.

I returned my unfired pistol to my holster and backed out of the kitchen. Outside, sirens wailed as more police units responded to the 'shots fired' call.

Jill trotted to my side as I leaned against Vic's car. "Are you okay?" she asked.

"I'm fine. And you?"

"I'm a bit rattled, but good. What happened? Why did Vic go for his gun? He didn't have a chance."

"It's called suicide by cop. Vic knew the situation was hopeless, and he didn't like the prospect of spending the rest of his life in prison."

"What a selfish…" Jill paused. "Everett is going to need some time. He shot twice."

"He'll have Laney to help him talk through the trauma."

Van Horn walked out, his head shaking. "Helluva thing."

"Yep."

"Did either of you discharge your firearm?"

I shook my head. "Neither Jill nor I fired."

Van Horn cocked his head. "Why not? He was going for his gun."

"I would've backed you up if you'd missed. Once you guys fired, there was no need. Vic was no longer a threat."

Van Horn's adrenaline was fading. He leaned against the house as if just standing was more than he could handle. "I've never fired my pistol except on the range."

I nodded. "Most cops retire without ever discharging their weapon at someone."

Poquette walked out with Everett and the female deputy. "Liz is going to take the recorder back to the courthouse and have it transcribed. It recorded everything from the time she sat down at the table with Mischkes until she turned it off after Vic's shooting."

"Good job, Liz," Van Horn said. He looked at Jill and me. "I guess we can release Belinda."

Jill and Van Horn took Everett and Liz aside and spoke to them while Everett nodded. Jill glanced at me and gave me a 'thumbs up' sign behind her back. I assume that meant their pep talk was helping Everett deal with his role in Vic's shooting. I overheard the sheriff say, "That shooting was hard on all of us. I've never fired my weapon anywhere but on the range until today. Hell, you'll probably never have to draw your pistol again unless you stumble across a rabid beaver!"

Motion in the shop door caught my eye as the dog's head appeared. Her tongue hung from her mouth as she panted. I knelt down and called to her, "Here girl. Come."

Mischke's dog tentatively stepped out of the shop, then stopped. I encouraged her, "Come on. It's okay, girl." She slowly crossed from the shop to where I was kneeling and stopped just out of my reach. "We're done shooting. It's okay."

Poquette broke away from the group of deputies and squatted down next to the traumatized dog. "Hey, girl. It's okay. No one else is going to shoot."

"Do you know anyone who needs a quiet, gun-shy dog?" I asked.

Poquette looked at the gathering deputies, who all shook their heads. "Aw, hell. My wife will kill me, but my kids would love having a second dog to play with."

Beyond the group of deputies, I saw Everett walking toward his pickup with a bit more confidence. Van Horn and Jill walked back to Poquette and me. "Thanks for talking to Everett, Sheriff. He's going to have nightmares."

Van Horn snorted. "Hell, I'll have nightmares, and I didn't even like Vic!"

I steered the sheriff and Poquette to the corner of the house and away from the other deputies. The dog followed Poquette, apparently understanding that he was going to be her BFF.

I scratched the dog's head and said, "Belinda's going to need some counseling. After thinking that her father had killed Flacowski for all these years, she's going to struggle with the news that Vic fired the killing shot. Then, she'll have to process the deaths of her parents."

"Helluva thing," Van Horn said, shaking his head. "Who would've thought Vic would kill two people."

"He's killed at least three people," I corrected, "if you count Flacowski."

"Vic was one of us."

I shook my head. "Vic was using his connections with you and the local cops. I suspect he's been passing the information he gleans from his coffee with the guys for years to tip off someone who's either been distributing or smuggling drugs."

"That might explain some things," Van Horn said to Poquette.

After a moment of consideration, Poquette said, "That would explain why we can nab a couple of the small fries, but the big players always seem to slip away."

Jill and Liz had a conversation away from the rest of us. Together, they approached the sheriff. "We'd like to be the ones to tell Belinda about her parent's deaths," Liz said.

Still rattled by what had transpired, the sheriff nodded. "Oh, shit. I'd completely forgotten about Belinda. Go ahead."

"I'll be at the sheriff's office when you come in to make your statement," Jill said before getting into the county SUV with Liz.

Poquette slapped his thigh. The dog came to him and nuzzled his hand. "I'll be there after I introduce our new pup to the family."

# Chapter 17

The rest of the day and evening were a whirlwind. We listened to Liz's recording of Mischke's shooting, which clearly revealed Vic as the shooter. Jill, Everett, and I were interviewed and signed the transcribed formal statements.

After a silent trip from the sheriff's office to the resort, Everett dropped us off at our cabin. He looked as tired as I felt. "Can I tell Laney what happened?"

"In general terms," I suggested. "She might be freaked out about your part in the shooting at Mischke's place."

After staring at his shoes for a moment while the mosquitoes swarmed around us, he nodded. "I suppose this might be the point where she comes to grips with what it means to be dating a cop, or we go our separate ways."

Jill and I nodded, knowing there was nothing we could add to that factual assessment of their relationship. We walked to the cabin, brushed the mosquitoes away as best we could, and walked inside. After flopping onto the bed, Jill said, "I'm hungry, but I don't think I could face the questions we'll get if we eat in the lodge."

I picked up a laminated menu from under the phone. "Room service will deliver anything on the lodge's menu."

"Order a pizza while I shower."

Our pizza arrived twenty minutes later. A young woman I'd seen around the lodge delivered it with a cold liter bottle of Pepsi. She hesitated for a second after I signed a room charge slip for the pizza and handed her a five-dollar tip. "You guys were at Mischke's?"

"Only as observers."

"Everett talked to Laney. She told the cook she had an emergency and needed to leave. Do you know what that was about?"

"I don't have a clue."

Jill swatted the mosquitoes that flew in during the pizza exchange while I opened the pizza box on the desk. "You avoided her question adeptly."

"I have no idea what Everett is going to say to Laney."

"You're not having beer?" Jill asked.

"I've decided to skip alcohol."

Jill slid a slice of pizza onto a napkin and took a bite. "The AA guys in Kentucky got you thinking?"

My cell phone rang before I answered Jill's question. Expecting to hear my boss' voice, I was surprised when Rachel said, "Hi. Do you guys have plans for tomorrow morning?"

"Not other than sleeping late and eating breakfast."

"Be at the fire hall at ten o'clock. We're diving."

"You don't need us..."

"Jill didn't tell you about calling me after her discussion with Liz and Belinda?"

I looked at Jill, who was eating a slice of pizza and flipping through television stations. "Tell me what?"

"On the night of Flacowski's murder, Belinda watched her father, Vic, and Flacowski arguing from her bedroom window. She said Flacowski was shot while standing on the dock. She couldn't tell who had shot because it was pouring rain, plus Vic and her dad were dressed in dark clothing and were backlit by the light."

"Okay. What's that got to do with us diving tomorrow?"

"Jill thinks we'll be able to recover parts of Flacowski's skull in the water near the side of the dock."

"Rachel..."

Jill looked up from the pizza, apparently understanding the call. "Let's dive. I'd like closure."

"Liz and Belinda are meeting us at the dock."

I looked at Jill, who raised her eyebrows and said, "Well?"

Knowing I'd been outvoted, I replied, "I'll call Everett."

"No need. He'll pick you up at the usual place at the usual time."

I disconnected the call and picked up a slice of pizza. "You knew about this?"

"I didn't *know* anything except that Liz was going to talk to the sheriff and Rachel about making a dive at the dock. Apparently, they made a plan."

"You'll freeze."

"I think the closure will compensate."

"What if we don't find anything?" I asked.

"Belinda was specific about what happened and where it happened. This shouldn't take long."

"A short-range shotgun blast is messy. You saw what happened to Peggy Mischke. There might be fragments of Flacowski all the way to Canada."

Jill shook her head. "Belinda saw the men kick something into the water. She thought it was a small duffel bag." Jill paused. "Liz and I spoke after Belinda was taken to a motel. We think what they kicked off the dock might've been part of Flacowski."

* * *

We were suited up and in the boat by 10:30. Everett and I helped Rachel launch the boat in I-Falls, then we motored to Mischke's dock. Everett agreed to meet us at

Mischke's where Liz and Belinda were waiting.

"Are you up to diving?" I asked Jill.

"It'll be cold. I'll deal with it."

"I'm more concerned about your shoulder. You stood well away from the boat when we launched it, which makes me think you're hurting."

"Don't expect me to do any heavy lifting."

We tied up and stepped onto the dock where Flacowski had been shot. The dock's weathered cedar planks looked old enough to have been in place at the time of the shooting. Reading my mind, Liz commented, "I don't suppose we'd be able to recover any of Flacowski's blood from the wood after thirty-some years of storms and aging."

Rachel was focused on the dive and was setting out gear. "Let's get going. I have to work this afternoon."

While Jill and Rachel strapped on tanks and weights, I approached Belinda. "Do you know where Flacowski and the shooter were standing?"

Belinda looked shell-shocked. Having been mentally elsewhere, my question jarred her back to the present. "Um, what?"

"You told Jill and Liz you'd watched the shooting from your bedroom window. Point out where Flacowski and the shooter were standing."

Belinda pointed to a second-floor window. "My bedroom was there." Turning back toward us, she considered the dock. "Dad's boat was always tied up to these cleats. I think Dad was trying to get Will into the boat, so he was standing about even with the tie-down cleats. Vic was closer to shore."

I stepped to the position I thought the shooter might've taken. Raising my arm, I pointed toward Liz, who was standing between the cleats. "So, the shot would've been taken at about this angle, toward the end of the dock?"

Belinda considered the question and shrugged. "I suppose about there. It's kind of hard to tell when I'm standing down here." She froze as recognition swept over her. "Dad was with Will next to the boat. Vic was farther away. He shot Will."

I climbed into the dive boat and said, "I think we should start here, near the boat, then swim towards the end of the dock."

Rachel was ready to dive. "Let's do it!"

Without fanfare, Rachel stepped over the gunwale and dropped backwards into the water. Jill pulled her mask into place and adjusted the straps. "We're looking for a skull?"

"More likely bone fragments."

Jill stepped over the gunwale and lowered herself using only her good arm. Then, with a splash, she dropped backwards into the water.

It took me another minute or two to get the gear on and adjusted. When I dropped into the water, I was stung by the cold hitting my exposed face and wrists. It took a moment for me to get oriented and locate Jill and Rachel.

With hand signals, Rachel indicated she wanted me to swim along the edge of the dock. She placed Jill a few feet away from the dock, then took a position a few feet beyond that. With all of us arranged, she signaled for us to swim away from shore. I spooked a school of crappies that were hiding under the dock.

After swimming less than five feet, Jill signaled that she'd spotted something on the lakebed. Rachel swam over to her, then dove down a few feet to the bottom. She was creating swirling clouds of sediment by the time I arrived. After a minute, the water had cleared enough to see the row of teeth in a mandible. Rachel carefully inserted her fingers under the jaw and pulled it out of the sandy bottom. After placing it in her dive bag, she gestured for Jill and me to "comb" the surrounding bottom with our fingers.

The disturbance caused another cloud of sediment that quickly obscured my vision. With slow, deliberate sweeps, I felt through the sand. I found a few stones, then felt something irregular with an almost sawtooth edge. Sliding my fingers under the piece, I lifted but felt unexpected resistance as the lake bottom muck held the piece. Using my left hand to brace myself, I pulled harder and wiggled the piece. With an unexpected swirl of sediment, the bottom let go of the piece, causing me to turn and rise.

I used my fins and free hand to level myself. Once back in control, I turned the piece as the murky sediment settled. Jill joined me, curious about what had created all of the commotion. She recoiled slightly when the exposed eye sockets became visible in the large piece of skull I'd found.

Rachel joined us and cocked her head while examining the piece. After a moment of consideration, she motioned for us to surface. Liz and the others were a few feet away, having a conversation. The sound of us breaking through the surface caused them all to turn in our direction.

Sensitive to Belinda's look of dread, I slipped the partial skull into my dive bag and held it up to Everett. I pulled my mask off and nodded to Liz, who perceived that we'd recovered something. "I think Belinda should wait for us in the warm SUV."

Liz wrapped her arms around Belinda's shoulders and turned her toward shore. "Let's take a walk, shall we?"

Everett peeked into the bag, then asked me, "Are you going to keep looking?"

"Rachel, how much more bottom time do we have?"

Checking her dive watch, she replied, "It's really shallow here, less than six feet. We've got at least another fifteen minutes of air."

"Jill, are you okay with another fifteen minutes of cold water?" I asked.

"Yes."

We continued the murky search, barely able to discern each other's position as we combed through the bottom sediment. The remaining pieces we recovered were smaller, a testament to the force of the shotgun blast and Will Flacowski's instant death.

I had half a dozen pieces of skull and a couple of teeth in my bag when Rachel signaled for us to return to the dock. After taking off our gear, we handed the dive bags to Everett. Rachel poured cocoa as Everett set the pieces on the boat deck.

After arranging the recognizable pieces, Everett stood back. "We need someone good at jigsaw puzzles to put the rest of this together."

"That'll be a great project for the medical examiner and his assistant," I replied.

Jill's hands were wrapped around the cocoa cup, absorbing the heat. "I think we found about three-quarters of the bones and teeth."

Rachel moved a couple of the pieces around, matching the irregular edges together when she found them. "I think we've got more than three quarters of the skull. I don't think we'd find half of the rest in another two dives."

"The law of diminishing returns," I observed. "You get about eighty percent of the return in the first twenty percent of the effort. I don't think additional searching would be a good use of your time."

Rachel smiled. "Wow, a cop who realizes my time has value. I'm impressed."

Jill turned and hugged our fellow diver. "You're invaluable."

"I've never been hugged by a cop before, either."

"Yeah, that's a once-in-a-lifetime occurrence. You wouldn't want most of the deputies to hug you anyway."

"Everett, gather all of the pieces and put them into an evidence bag. We'll let the sheriff's people deliver them to the Duluth ME."

Rachel topped off our cocoa as Everett walked away with the dive bags. "This is a story I'll be telling my grandchildren." Checking her watch, she said, "We've got to head back, or I'll be late for work."

I cast off the lines as Rachel started the outboard motor, then I sat alongside Jill as we motored back to the I-Falls boat launch. "How is your shoulder?"

"The doctor told me to ice it. Right now, it's numb."

* * *

After helping Rachel with the boat and gear, Jill and I changed into our street clothes. Once we were dressed, we found

Rachel sitting in the firehouse kitchen with steaming cups of cocoa.

"Thanks for everything," I said.

"By the way, I updated your PADI files, showing that you were recertified."

"I'm not sure whether to thank or curse you," Jill replied. "I hope I never have to dive again, and certainly not to recover bones or a body."

Everett arrived as we finished our cocoa. "The sheriff wants you guys to come back to his office and make a formal statement about recovering the skull."

I sighed. "I somehow knew that was coming."

"Let's not rush back," Jill suggested. "Rachel, do you have enough time to join us for lunch?"

After glancing at the clock, she nodded. "The Knothole Café has great chili. It might be just what we need to take the chill off."

* * *

We spent the afternoon with Liz, Poquette, and Van Horn. After taking our statements, we went to a conference room, and Van Horn closed the door. "If Vic was informing the druggies about our operations, we should start having better luck with our arrests."

"Who is the guy with the dog on Mischke's road?"

Van Horn glanced at the door, as if making sure no one else had entered. "This information stays in the room. He's the latest in a string of undercover RCMP agents who've occupied that house. They all claim to be children or relatives of the original owners."

"Does the dog stay, or does he go back with the latest agent?" Jill asked.

"There's always a dog there. I think they're connected to the individuals. Hell, maybe they always send a K-9 officer. I've never asked. All I know is that we've been told to stay clear of that place."

Van Horn held out his hand. "It's been a pleasure to work with you guys. Everett has always been someone we could rely on for backup when we needed him. I wasn't sure what to expect when you two showed up."

We shook hands with everyone in the room, then exited to the Park Service pickup with Everett. "We're eating supper at the lodge. Why don't you bring Laney over, and we'll chat while we eat the walleye special?"

"Laney says she eats the lodge food all of the time. She'd rather eat a frozen pizza than have another walleye special."

"Yeah," Jill said, nodding, "I would get tired of the walleye if I ate it weekly."

Everett dropped us at our cabin, then drove over to Laney's place.

"Do you need to change, or can we go right over to the lodge?" I asked Jill.

"I'm not going to change, but I need a couple of ibuprofen." I swatted mosquitoes until she came out with two pills in her hand. "It says to take them with a meal."

Megan waved to us as soon as we walked in, then pointed to an empty high-top table near the kitchen. I gave her a nod, and we threaded our way through the crowd. A guy turned away from his table and bumped into me. "Sorry. You must not have seen me signaling I was going to back up," he joked.

"No harm done," I replied.

Focusing on me for the first time, he stopped. "Hey, you're the cop who's been talking to Sertich, right?"

"Yeah, we've had a couple of conversations," I replied as I tried to edge past him.

"Was he really a hockey player?"

"I guess so. I'm not local, so I couldn't swear to it."

The guy looked past me to where Lyle was sitting at the end of the bar with his hands wrapped around a beer mug. "He's a little kooky, but, WOW, he took his team to two high school championships and was offered a pro contract. That's really something."

I was tempted to say that was nothing compared to what he experienced in Vietnam, then decided the guy really wouldn't care. "Yes, Lyle is the real deal. A real star."

Jill was seated at the table when I arrived. "What did the drunk want?"

"He's a fan of Lyle's."

Jill looked past me at Lyle and sighed. "I'm going to invite him over."

I must've smirked. "You're inviting Booger over. He might sneeze on you."

"Shush!" she said before walking over to the end of the bar. Lyle was focused on his beer until Jill touched his arm. His rheumy eyes looked up at her, starting a transformation. He went from a sad drunk to a smiling old guy. They shared a few words, then he shook his head before waving at me. Jill leaned close to whisper something to him, followed by a kiss on his cheek.

Lyle straightened up as if the decades were slipping away, returning him to an earlier version of himself. He touched Jill's arm and said something I couldn't hear. He watched her walk back to our table, then nodded to the bartender, who was grinning.

"What did you say to him?"

"I thanked him for helping us."

I turned and nodded to Lyle, mouthing, "Thanks."

A smile spread across his face, and he nodded back. I motioned for him to join us, but he shook his head, holding up his beer as if it was all he was interested in.

"Did you tell him we found Flacowski?"

"He already knew that. He'd heard we'd shot Vic and told me not to let the dreams haunt me."

Megan interrupted us, taking our beverage and dinner orders. When she left, I whispered, "I bet the nightmares still haunt Lyle. He experienced hell in Vietnam."

"Can we talk about something happier?" Jill asked as she reached for my hand.

Megan rushed back with Jill's wine and my Pepsi. Seeing us holding hands, she smiled. "Romance is blossoming in the Park Service."

"You know that we're married, right?" I asked.

"I assumed, but didn't KNOW," she said. "Then, there's Laney and Ev."

"Their romance is blossoming?" Jill asked.

"I don't know where Ev's head is, but Laney's all in."

The usual chatter and laughter covered Karen Swift's entrance into the lodge restaurant. Jill noticed her walking through the maze of tables. "Over here!"

Karen pulled an empty stool over from a nearby table. Smiling, she looked at our beverages. "I thought you two would be drinking champagne to celebrate the closure of the case."

Jill's smile was forced, and she stared at me as if saying, *"You explain this."*

"We don't celebrate when our cases end in deaths."

Karen's smile faded, and she blew out a breath. "Yeah. I understand that."

After delivering two platters of walleye to a neighboring table, Megan turned to us. "I see you've collected another ranger. What would you like to drink?"

"White wine, please, and I'll have the walleye platter."

With Megan gone, Karen leaned close. "Can you tell me what happened? Everett has been filling me in, but I think there's more depth to the story than he grasps."

Taking advantage of the ambient noise to cover her hushed voice, Jill explained who the victim was, the story of his demise, the recovery, the role of Lyle Sertich and Karl Peterson in unraveling the motive, and the ugly scene at Mischke's resulting in the death of three people. Karen listened attentively, asking for clarification when needed. Megan delivered Karen's wine and told us our meals would be up next.

Karen leaned back, digesting all she'd heard. "I understand why you're not drinking champagne. Are all of your cases this complicated and grisly?"

Jill drew a breath and leaned forward. "Your efforts to provide a safe and entertaining park are sometimes upturned by sociopaths. Luckily, that doesn't happen very often. When problems arise, your law enforcement rangers deal with ninety-nine percent of them quickly. We only get involved when things get beyond their capabilities."

Shaking her head, Karen grimaced. "Somehow, I thought you two would be more...hands-off. You know, like consultants who stand back and advise."

"Ideally, that would be our role," I conceded. "We have to be prepared to deal with whatever comes up. Once the sheriff's department got involved, they took over the heavy lifting, and we stepped back in a supporting role."

The arrival of our dinners interrupted the discussion. Megan checked on our beverages and confirmed that we had all we needed. When she left, Karen said, "I talked to Dutch Van Horn."

"And?" I asked.

"Officially, he's going to announce the solution of the murder and the shootout as his department's resolution of a murder investigation. Unofficially, he conceded that they would never have cracked the case if not for you two."

# Epilogue

Jill's phone rang as I walked into the bathroom to shave. She was dressed and zipping her suitcase when I was through. "Who called?"

"Susie said Mom fell down last night. She drove them to the ER. There are no broken bones, but the ER doctor referred Mom to a neurologist and suggested she get a medical alert bracelet. She might have had a TIA."

"TIA?"

"I guess that's a mini-stroke. There are no lingering effects, but it might be a warning that something more serious is on the horizon."

"I'm glad Susie was there," I said as I chose my travel clothes.

Jill hugged me and rested her head on my shoulder. "I'm sad not to be there for them. On the other hand, Susie's presence on the ranch makes me more comfortable."

"We can defer our South Dakota retirement?" I replied, a little too enthusiastically.

Jill sighed. "At least until Susie finds a job."

"The market for middle-aged forestry managers is probably saturated. Susie might be on the ranch for a long time."

Jill and I walked over to the lodge for breakfast. Laney darted away from the table she was bussing and brought us coffee. Once the coffee was poured, she stood next to the table, apparently unsure of what to say.

"I'll have the usual," I said, breaking the ice.

"Oatmeal with raisins for me," Jill added.

Laney left for the kitchen with our orders.

"I wonder how much she knows about what happened at Mischke's place?" Jill asked.

"We reminded Everett not to share any pillow talk. On the other hand, he needed to talk through what happened, and he hinted the shooting might be the tipping point in their relationship."

Jill nodded her agreement. "He needed a sympathetic ear. Laney is either that person, or she isn't."

Max Davidson walked in, spotted us, and took a seat at the table. "You two have had quite a week."

"I'm sad it turned out the way it did," I replied. "The Mischkes didn't need to die."

Max sighed, "I feel terrible."

"You weren't responsible for their deaths," I said. "That's on Vic English."

Max nodded but appeared unconvinced. "Laney told me she's not going back to college. She asked if she could continue working and stay in the cabin over the winter. We can always use some help with snowmobilers and ice fishermen, so I told her yes."

"How many charity cases are you caring for?" Jill asked.

Davidson seemed surprised by the question. "Charity cases?"

"Lyle, Karl, and now Laney."

"Lyle and Karl are my in-house entertainment."

Jill smiled and said, "Ah, Lyle and Karl are in the resort's retirement plan, and Laney will earn her wages."

"Our retirement plan. I like that." Max signaled Laney for a cup of coffee and asked, "Are you two flying back to Texas today?"

"That's our plan."

"Could I interest you in another day here, on me? I'd personally take you fishing." When we didn't immediately respond, he added, "I feel like I owe you something."

"Thanks, but we were just doing our jobs."

Jill nodded. "I've got dying flowers in Texas, and our boss expects our expense vouchers and trip reports to be submitted promptly."

Max Davidson leaned close to Jill and squeezed her hand as he whispered something to her. Laney showed up with his coffee and our meal a minute later. After Laney left, Davidson stood and picked up his coffee mug. "Thanks for what you've done."

"As I said, we did our jobs," I replied.

Davidson winked at Jill, then smiled at me. "Some of what you did was above and beyond the call of duty."

I unfolded my napkin as Max walked away with his mug. "What did he whisper to you?"

"He asked if I planned to open a counseling service. Apparently, Laney has been bragging about the great guidance I've been providing."

Everett rushed in looking like he was late. He sat next to Jill and smiled at her in a way that said something she'd suggested had worked out. Looking at me, he asked, "Is there anything you need to do before I take you to the airport?"

"We're packed. All we need to do is load our bags into the truck."

Laney walked over and asked,. "Morning, Ev, can I get you something?"

"No thanks, I've got to drive Jill and Doug to the airport."

Jill stood and said, "I'll help you load up while Doug settles our bill." She said goodbye to Laney, then she and Everett walked out of the lodge.

Laney waited until they were out of the door, then she turned to me. "Everett was a mess last night. Did he really shoot that guy?"

"I can't comment."

Laney stared at me for a second, then asked, "How can I help him get past this? I mean, he was really a mess last night."

"Listen. Don't judge him. Don't try to *fix* him."

"It wasn't like Vic was a nice guy. Why is Ev so...messed up?"

"Vic was a human being, and we're taught that every life is precious. Killing someone, anyone, is contrary to everything we were taught in Sunday school. It messes up your head. You never get over it entirely."

"Have you...?"

"I still have nightmares. Jill snuggles with me and listens."

"I told Everett about...my situation at school..." Laney looked at me like she expected me to finish her sentence.

I put my arm around her shoulders and pulled her close. "Have you seen a counselor?"

She nodded. "At the University. I didn't tell her everything. I was too...ashamed because I felt like I'd caused some of it."

"There is no excuse for a guy hurting someone he claims to love. None."

Laney hugged me and said, "You and Jill are special people. I wish my mom and dad were more like you."

I chuckled. "We're dealing with the easy part of your life. We didn't have to change your diapers or sell Girl Scout cookies."

"Mom says the 'terrible twos' were nothing compared to the 'know-it-all teens.'"

"And now, you're at the point where Mom and Dad are smart and important."

"We're getting there." Laney paused and wiped her eyes. "They're coming up after Labor Day. It'll be the first time they'll meet Ev."

"If they're smart, they'll come to love him as much as he loves you."

"Do your parents love Jill?"

"There's only my mom, and she loves Jill more than she loves me."

"How long did it take for Jill's parents to accept you?"

"That jury is still out."

Laney gave me a playful shove. "She says they think you're very special."

Jill was waiting for me outside the lodge. "Did you and Laney talk?"

"You set me up."

"Laney needed to hear some things from a male perspective."

"You told her your parents think I'm special."

"You are special."

"I'm not sure your dad thinks so."

Jill put her arm around my waist and pulled me close as we walked to the pickup where Everett was waiting. "Uncle Chet said every time we leave, he and Dad drive to the Moose Lodge and Dad spends the whole evening telling his buddies 'Doug' stories. He's so proud of you, he's busting at the seams."

"I don't believe you."

Holding up three fingers, she replied. "Scout's honor."

"You were never a scout."

"Okay, on your 4Her's honor."

"There's no such thing..."

Everett shook his head when we got into the truck. "What are you two laughing about?"

"Doug's jealous because his mom likes me better than she likes him."

"Is that true?" he asked me.

"Absolutely! Jill returns Mom's phone calls and listens to her talk about health issues. In my mother's eyes, Jill's a saint."

Everett grinned. "Laney and I think she's someone special."

Jill patted him on the shoulder. "Thanks, Everett. At least some people appreciate me."

"I appreciate you, too. I married you!"
Everett broke out laughing. "I hope I'm
as funny as you two are when I get old."

The End

Dean Hovey is the award-winning and best-selling author of three mystery series. He uses his scientific background, travel, extensive research, and consultants to add reality and depth to his stories. One reader said Dean's characters are like people he'd like to invite over for a beer and discussion. Hovey's Doug Fletcher mysteries follow U.S. National Park Service investigators Doug and Jill Fletcher as their investigations take them to national parks from coast to coast. The Whistling Pines mysteries (co-written with Anne Flagge) are humorous cozies set in a northern Minnesota senior residence, following Peter Rogers, the Whistling Pines recreation director, as he stumbles through the investigation of murders in his small town. The Pine County mysteries (co-written with D.L. Dixen) follow sheriff's deputies Pam Ryan, Floyd Swenson, and CJ Jensen as they investigate murders in rural Minnesota. Dean and his wife split their year between northern Minnesota and Arizona.

## *Other Dean L. Hovey mysteries from BWL Publishing Inc.*

### *Whistling Pines cozies*
Whistling up a Ghost
Whistling Pirates
Whistling Bake Off
Whistling Artist
Whistling Fireman
Whistling Wedding
Whistling Librarian (with Anne Flagge)

### *Doug Fletcher mysteries*
Stolen Past
Washed Away
Dead in the Water
Death in Shifting Sands
Devils Fall
Prairie Menace
Down River
Burnt Evidence
Gator Bait
Grave Survey
Dead End Trail
The Last Rodeo
Peril in Paradise
Western Justice
Strung Out to Die
Medora Murder
A Bourbon to Die For

***Pine County Mysteries***
Killer Secrets
Deadly Mixture
Fatal Business
Taxed to Death
Conflict of Interest
Skidded and Skunked (with D.L. Dixen)

***Canadian Historical Mysteries***
Bad Omen: Nunavut (with John
Wisdomkeeper)